REAL
Time

BOOK ONE IN THE TIME FOR LOVE SERIES

Wendy Olher
Thanks for
support

JEANINE BINDER

Jeanine Binder

08/2016

First Edition. Printed in the United States of America.
ISBN-13: 978-1500914141 | ISBN-10: 1500914142

Editing by Juli's Elite Editing
www.facebook.com/JulisEliteEditing

Proofreading by Sallyann Cole

Cover & Formatting by Rene Folsom with Phycel Designs
www.Phycel.com

DEDICATION

A big thank you to my husband, EJ, and my daughter, Juli. Thank you for believing in me.

TABLE OF CONTENTS

CHAPTER ONE

Nick Marshall planted his booted foot onto the desk in front of him, taking a long drag off the cigarette in his left hand and closing his eyes as he laid his head back on the chair. *This cannot be that bloody hard*, he thought, exhaling and opening his eyes to watch the smoke swirl over his head. In a city the size of Los Angeles, how difficult can it be to find ONE person who can play the piano? Nick was starting to get anxious and more than simply irritated. He had been auditioning to replace Marcus Daily, his keyboard player of fifteen years. Marcus had retired in the spring, stating he wanted to be closer to home, closer to his kids. Nick appreciated his sentiments and sent him off with a bang - a new job at the studio which would accomplish that. Now the bang was in his head as a headache continued to grow through a well of sheer frustration. He'd thought this would be an easy task – now he was three weeks away from his six-month US tour and no keyboard player in sight.

Nick was forty-five years old, six-foot-four, blond hair, and a body to go with it. In the past thirty years he had become a solid force in the music world: twenty-five gold records, twenty-three platinum records, fourteen double platinum records, one diamond record, and sold out shows wherever he went. What started out as a career as a humble guitar player had turned into quite an entourage. To make a Nick Marshall show required six band members, including himself, twelve roadies to put up and take down the stage, two bodyguards for Nick and a security force of six for the rest of the band, two bus drivers, two truck drivers, and a very overworked manager.

And it was the overworked manager, Mickey Simon, who came over with the next resume for Nick to look over. Once they had figured out about half the applicants couldn't actually read music, it cut down the number of people applying for the position and Mickey was able to screen those out. But after almost three days, Nick was starting to be convinced he would be better off hiring a guitar player and playing the damn keyboards himself. Not something he wanted to do, but he was not about to hire some twenty year old who thought he could make an electronic keyboard 'sing.' Most of them froze when he pointed to the baby grand piano in the corner and asked them to play something.

"Here's the next one," Mickey said, handing him the resume.

"Great. How bad do you think this one will be?" Nick asked, with a cynical tone.

Mickey had been his manager since the beginning and he knew Nick well. He knew Nick's patience for this was just about at its end. "To be honest, this one has the talent. But there's a catch."

"There's always a catch, mate," he agreed, putting out the cigarette. "What is it?"

"It's a woman," he answered. "I know you usually don't screen women just because it's a pain in the arse. But if you look at her resume, she has lots of talent. And experience."

Nick scanned the paper. Katelyn Thomas was the name on it. He cocked his head a little, trying to recall where he had heard her name. "Mickey, right now if they could read music and play the piano, I'd hire a chimpanzee."

Mickey laughed as he walked away to show her in to the studio. Nick went back to the resume and saw she had been working as a studio musician for the past six years. Satellite Records. *That's why her name is so familiar*. Nick had never used her services – up until now he didn't need a stand-in keyboard player for his records. *This would be interesting but complicated,* he thought. He wasn't so worried about her being a woman. He could work around the issue although it would mean changing some arrangements at hotels and things, but Mickey was a genius at adjustment work. No, the parts he wanted to avoid were the rumors and the accusations she was sleeping with him to get the job. It would be the first headline on the tabloids and would follow him from city to city. Contrary to the said tabloids, Nick stayed away from the young girls and the only one night stand he could even remember was when he was sixteen.

The woman following behind Mickey was pretty and Nick was glad to see she at least appeared older than twenty. She had auburn hair pulled into a ponytail, going down her back, green eyes, and looked to be about five-foot-nine. She was dressed well in a pair of nice jeans, nice blouse, jacket, and stylish boots. She appeared confident and when she made eye contact with him, she had a professional look on her face. There was no hint she even knew who Nick was. It was nice to see a woman who didn't want to fawn in his presence.

"Katelyn Thomas," Mickey said as an introduction. "Nick Marshall."

Nick put his hand out and she put her hand in his. "I'm pleased to meet you, Katelyn."

"Kate, please," she said. "It's good to finally meet you. I've heard lots about you from other musicians I have worked with."

"Hopefully it's all good," he answered.

"Most of the time," she replied with a smile.

Nick liked her smile. Matter of fact there wasn't much about her he didn't like so far. "You do studio work?"

She nodded. "For the past six years I've been working for Satellite Records. I'm finishing up Jason Doonsby's latest album at the moment."

Nick was familiar with Jason's music. They sang different genres – Nick's was rock and roll and Jason's was country and western. They did not meet very often, but Jason was usually at the same parties and events Nick would occasionally attend.

"Well, here's the thing, love. My keyboard player retired and it's been the bloody devil trying to find a replacement. The biggest issues I'm having are either they don't read music or they only seem to be able to work with electronic keyboards. So if I pointed over there to the piano and asked you to play something, could you?"

Kate took her jacket off and laid it on the chair next to Nick's and walked over to the white baby grand piano. She paused for a moment, hearing music in her head then sat down on the bench. She took a deep breath before she started into some lively Chopin, moving into some well-known Mozart, and jazzed it up by playing some modern pieces – Burt Bacharach, Billy Joel, Elton John, and even played the chorus for one of Nick's better known ballads. Nick sat in his chair mesmerized. Mickey wasn't kidding when he said she had the talent. She made the piano sing and he was startled back to the here and now when she stopped, turning to look at him. "Enough?"

Without speaking, he picked up some of the sheet music on the desk and brought it over, sitting next to her on the piano bench. Each piece he put in front of her she would take a moment to look at it and then would play like she had done so all of her music career. Nick put his best known song, the one he needed the piano for, the one he even hauled a piano around the country for, in front of her. She took about two minutes, as she did with the others, and played it perfectly with no mistakes and no hesitation. In the middle of it, Nick got up and started to pace the room, thinking. He knew, without a doubt, he couldn't let her go – he had to hire her, no matter what happened with the press or the fans. He had never heard his music played with such beauty before. He saw Mickey watching through the sound booth windows and he motioned for him to come back in. Nick whispered something to him and then Nick turned back to Kate. Mickey walked back out of the studio quickly.

"I have no idea why, love," Nick began, "because you're definitely over qualified. But the job is yours if you want it."

"You're sure?" she asked, surprised. "I know my being a woman has to complicate things."

Nick sat back down on the bench beside her, picking up the music. "It's only a little complicated. And it's nothing I can't change with little or no effort." He put the music into a folder and set it back on the music stand. "Where did you learn to play like that?"

Nick saw a shadow cross her eyes and the excitement of winning the job starting to fade. "I trained as a concert pianist once," she replied. "I had great dreams of a magical career. It all went down the drain ten years ago with a broken hand."

She didn't say any more and Nick wasn't going to press her. It was obvious this was a bad memory and he didn't want to cause her pain in order to satisfy his curiosity. "How much more do you have left on Doonsby's album?"

"A couple more tracks. We should be finished this weekend or by mid-next week at the latest."

"And you're good to be gone for six months? That's how long this tour will be, then a three week vacation, followed by three months in Europe and Asia. After that, it calms down for a while until I get the rest of the music written for the next album. Then the chaos starts all over again."

"I have no commitments," she told him. "The lease on my condo is paid through the first of the year, so I don't have to worry about rent and things. I have a cat, but I can take her to my parent's house while I am gone."

Nick stood up, holding out his hand and Kate took it. "Then I welcome you aboard, love," he said, sealing the deal with a handshake. "Mickey will want to set up time to go over the contracts and all the Mickey-stuff with you."

She nodded. "No worries. I'm overwhelmed I got the job. I hadn't planned to audition for it."

"What changed your mind?"

She smiled, walking over to get her jacket. "One of the kids you turned down was Michael Grayson's son." Michael Grayson owned Satellite Records, this studio's biggest competitor. "Justin came storming back into the studio two days ago complaining you wouldn't even give him an audition because he didn't know how to play the piano; he had self-taught himself keyboards. So I thought, okay, I know how to play the piano and began to wonder if I had a shot. Justin was calling you all kinds of names by the way."

"I wasn't very nice to some of them, "he admitted. "I don't need a kid who can push buttons on a keyboard and become a one man band. One of my songs has a long piano solo and I suppose it could be played on electronics. However, I prefer the way a straight piano sets it off. "

"We see a lot of it at the studio – kids thinking an electronic keyboard makes them a musician. Real musicians appear to be few and far between. It's your music, Nick. Play it however you want."

"And I do." He started to walk with her out of the studio. "Is Monday good to come in and sign all the legal stuff?"

"I'll make the time," she promised.

Nick escorted her out of the studio and back to Mickey. Nick turned around, walking back to his desk and lighting another cigarette while waiting for Mickey to come back. After about five minutes, Mickey came back into the studio and sat down across from him. Nick was grinning from ear to ear. Just looking at him, Mickey had to laugh. "I'll start making the changes tomorrow. You realize this is going to cost you a bit."

"I don't care," Nick answered. "She is over qualified but I'm not looking a gift horse in the mouth."

"I saw her play once. Back when she was doing the concert stuff."

"Really? Where?"

"My niece was at Julliard at the same time. They had a performance and I went to watch. I always wondered what happened to her," Mickey said.

Nick put the cigarette out in the ash tray. "She said something about a broken hand. It really must have been a bad one if it would have put such a promising career away."

* * *

Kate was excited and a little stunned she had gotten the job. It was a known fact through the studio world that Nick Marshall's band did not have turnover very often and he rarely screened women. Kate thought it had to do with how the press would report the relationship – it added more fuel for the tabloid newspapers. She wasn't sure whether she got the job for her talent or for the anxiety of not having found someone much sooner in the audition process. Kate was glad for the change; not all the musicians on Satellite's roster were easy to work with and Kate always seemed to be assigned to those who tried her patience. They were never satisfied and the work became twice as hard as it had to be.

Driving the forty minutes back to the studio, Kate was going over in head exactly what she was going to say to Michael Grayson. She owed a lot to him – he didn't have to hire her when her dad had asked. It had given her a much needed boost in her confidence level because she hadn't been sure she was going to be able to continue with any kind of a music career. There had been a lot of damage and sometimes her hand would get stiff and sore when she played for long periods of time. Nick had seemed pleased with how well she played.

Once at the studio, she rode up to the eighth floor, where Michael's office was located. She had only been up there a couple of times since starting work there but had no difficulty finding it. His secretary, Rebecca, told her he was in a meeting for another hour but was willing to add her to his calendar for later in the afternoon. He only had thirty minutes available – Kate told her it would be more than enough time for what she needed. She left the area, going down to the studio to see where things were at for Jason's album.

Jason was one of those difficult artists to work with. He was never content it appeared, with anything which didn't take at least five or six retries.

He was a big hit with most of the women in the studio, except for Kate, and he would spend lots of time trying to convince her to go out with him. Kate always turned him down, which only seemed to spur him to try harder. She had tried on numerous records to trade the shifts with one of the other keyboard players, so she wouldn't have to deal with him. Next thing Kate knew, she was permanently assigned to his music; this told her Jason had thrown a fit to Michael.

The red warning light was off on the door for studio B, so she opened the door, walking quietly into the sound booth. Jason's backup singers were on the studio floor, telling Kate the vocals were being done and she wasn't needed. This was helpful to her peace of mind; she was not looking forward to the conversation she was going to have in about thirty minutes with her boss, and she was not in a good mood to deal with Jason. Thankfully, she only had two songs left and she planned to get those done quickly, especially since she would be leaving with Nick in three weeks. Jason wasn't going to like it but there wasn't much he could do about it. Studio musicians were free to quit, same as any other employee. There was not a specified contract stating otherwise, which Kate knew there would be one with Nick.

At five minutes to the hour, Kate was back up on the eighth floor, waiting by Michael's office. The waiting room was nicely decorated with pretty artwork and there was a large salt-water aquarium along one wall with brightly colored fish. She loved to watch the clown fish as they swam in and out of the coral reef which was built in the middle of the tank. She felt like a ten year old watching all the fish intently until Rebecca interrupted her, telling her she could go into Michael's office.

Kate walked confidently into the office. Michael Grayson was about six-foot tall, around fifty-eight years old, and wore a three-piece Armani suit. Kate couldn't remember seeing him wear anything but nice suits, including a matching silk tie and usually a diamond pin. He smiled at her as she walked in; Kate's step-dad, Allen, was a good friend and she knew him fairly well. Michael motioned to one of the chairs in front of his desk and she sat down.

"What can I do for you, Kate?" Michael asked, starting their conversation.

"I came to give you my verbal resignation," Kate said, without preamble. "I'll have the written one on your desk in the morning."

"Resignation?" he echoed, surprised. "Why are you resigning?"

"I signed on with Nick Marshall this afternoon," Kate answered.

"With Empire Records?" Michael asked, thinking she was going there to do the same kind of studio work.

"No. Nick hired me to replace his keyboard player."

"Now I am surprised," Michael said, raising an eyebrow. "Nick doesn't audition women. At least he hasn't in the past."

"I think he was desperate," she replied smiling. "He said he'd been having issues finding a piano player. You and I both know playing keyboards isn't about playing the piano and he didn't want simply a keyboard player. One of the reasons he rejected Justin two days ago."

"I'll be sorry to see you go, Kate," he said seriously. "Artists ask for you by name to work on their records. I'm going to have some very disappointed folks."

"I wanted to tell you in person because you were my salvation six years ago when I really needed it. And I also need your help with getting Jason to finish the remaining keyboard tracks this week."

"I'll help, but I'm not looking forward to the conversation," Michael agreed. "When is Nick leaving?"

"Three weeks and I want to have a week free for vacation and things, since I will be six months on the road with him for the first tour. I need to get all my personal stuff in line so I can be gone for such a long stretch."

Michael stood up and held his hand out to her. Kate took it, shaking his hand. "I wish you the best, Kate," Michael said sincerely. "And if things don't work out with Nick, you are welcome back any time."

"I appreciate all you've done, Michael," she said smiling. "Good to know I have other options if this doesn't work out."

CHAPTER TWO

After two weeks, Kate was getting the hang of being out on the road. Get on the bus – sometimes all night – get to a hotel, stay two or three days and start the cycle anew. In the beginning, she kept track of what city they were in but by the time they got to New York City, at the middle of the tour, Kate had long since given up. It was one city after another, one hotel after another, and the venues were all pretty much the same. Most were large sports arenas which seated over forty-thousand so there were always large crowds on hand. A couple of times an additional show had been added and kept them an extra day which usually meant an all-nighter on the bus going to the next place.

Kate didn't mind the all-nighters because the bus was luxurious. It had plush couches in the front with a television, stereo, and six bunk style beds installed in the back. Usually after a long stretch, the beds even started to get comfortable because she was just too tired to care. Kate thought doing studio work had been difficult but she quickly found how out of scope her expectations had been. In spite of the hard work, long hours, and endless stretches of highway, she was enjoying herself. The other band members, Dave, Steve, Andy, and Trent, treated her like one of them instantly – playing practical jokes and including her in some of their escapades. The five of them would go down to the hotel bars after the show sometimes and hang out together, talking and having fun. Nick rarely joined them, as he got recognized easily and didn't like the crowds which seemed to magically appear. Kate felt like she had found a new home and a new family in the bargain.

She had been a little wary in the beginning that Nick or one of the guys might come onto her, try to get her in bed, but, surprisingly, they were consistently gentlemen around her. All but Nick and Trent were married. Trent treated her like a kid sister, even though Kate was older, and Nick didn't talk to her much. He spent most of his time with Mickey going over each coming show and usually shut himself up in his hotel room the rest of the time. So they made it easy for her to fit in, laugh and joke, and she usually beat them playing cards. She was cutthroat, showing no mercy, and they respected her, although they used swear words in interesting combinations when she would win the ante pot. The security guys treated her the same way. Maybe even more protective as this was their main job – to keep the band members safe, especially from over-zealous fans.

Kate was nervous at the first show but she was professional enough it wasn't noticeable. Nick was observant enough to come over and make sure she was good. One of the questions he forgot to ask when he auditioned her was whether or not she got stage fright. She told him she was fine and indeed she was. Based on where the keyboards were located, she got a good view of the musician Nick Marshall. Everything about him exuded strength and confidence. He wore black motorcycle boots – she had jokingly asked him before the first show if he even had a motorcycle, to which he had said yes. He did admit he'd had the boots longer than the bike, which made her laugh. Nick wore black pants and a sleeveless button down shirt, usually leaving two or three buttons open. His hair was growing out – it was past shoulder length and she suspected he wore it long during shows for the effect. 'The effect' consisted of a whole arena or stadium full of girls screaming his name. Kate had to admit he did provide a nice view, even though she didn't see him as more than her employer. For the rest of the band, Nick didn't care what was worn for performances – whatever was most comfortable on stage, as long as it looked nice.

The bus was currently stopped at a big hotel in Manhattan. Normally, the routine was for Mickey to hop out, go inside and register, while the bus would pull up to one of the back doors. Once Mickey came back, everyone would pile out, grab a suitcase, and head for their room. Whenever possible, Nick would reserve an entire floor just to maintain privacy and make it easier on security since no one but the maids were allowed up on that particular floor. This hotel had no apparent "back" door, so as soon as Mickey had the registration completed, everyone got off the bus, took a room key from him, and made their way through the gorgeous lobby. Kate was lagging behind, admiring the furnishings and the way it was all laid out when she heard her name called. She turned around, surprised to see her ex-husband standing there.

"Kevin," she answered hesitantly, as he walked over to her. Ten years had changed him; his dark brown hair had grayed around the temples and he looked fifty, not the thirty-two she knew he was.

"What are you doing here?" he asked, looking her over. It had been almost ten years since their divorce. She watched him as he looked her over, almost a leer in his eyes.

She nodded to the security guard who was waiting. "Go ahead, Brock," she told him. "I'll be okay." The security guard walked away but not completely out of sight. "I work for Nick Marshall these days," she said, turning back to Kevin. "We have three shows at the Garden." 'The Garden' obviously meant Madison Square Garden.

"That's a step down for you isn't it?" he asked, with a snide tone.

"I don't think so," she countered. "It's a lot of hard work. A lot harder than the studio work I'd been doing."

"And I'm sure the nights are hard too."

Kate started to see red, picking up his innuendo. Their year of marriage was filled with these types of comments and statements meant to demean her. "You didn't just insinuate I got the job because I'm sleeping with Nick or the band, did you?"

He started to laugh. "Well, if the shoe fits."

Without another word, Kate reached over and slapped him hard across the face. "How dare you! You have no right to criticize or judge me. I don't have to sleep around to get any job!"

She started to walk off but he angrily grabbed her arm. It was apparent a fight was about to ensue as Kevin raised his hand up to return the slap. Before he could connect, a large hand interfered, stopping him.

"Go on upstairs, Kate," Brock said quietly, staring Kevin down. Kate walked away toward the elevator. Once the door had closed, Brock released his grip. "I think the lady made herself clear. I advise you to stay away."

Brock walked away while Kevin remained standing there, angry at being stopped. He was going to follow him but thought better of it and walked over to the front desk. He asked for Kate's room number, but when he gave her name, they told him the hotel didn't have anyone registered by her name. He tried Nick also, but the desk clerk said she couldn't give him any of Nick's information, per the contract they had with the musician. *She'll have to come back out this way* he thought, moving over to a chair so that he could watch the elevator. *We will continue this when she comes back down*, Kevin thought, settling down to wait. It had been ten years but he had finally found her.

* * *

Up on the eighth floor, Kate's heart had stopped pounding from her encounter and she found her room easily. It was a suite with a sitting room, bathroom and bedroom – which was standard because Nick usually had one of the security people sleeping in the sitting room.   Sometimes there would be two bedrooms attached to one sitting room, but she was glad this one was a single. Kate tossed her suitcase in the corner and sat down in one of the chairs, still shaky from the brief exchange with Kevin. She hadn't seen him since the day he knocked her down the stairs of their apartment – her attorney had kept her from having to face him physically in court when they were going through the divorce. She had hoped after ten years he could at least be civil but it was obvious he was still angry. Kate didn't understand why this was directed at her – he had gotten the scholarship they had been competing over and the job with the London Philharmonic as a featured pianist. Matter of fact, their divorce should have helped as he'd been able to move to London with no strings attached. And he had a fabulous career with them, staying on after the internship.

Kate waited another thirty minutes to see if Brock, or even Nick, was going to show up pounding on her door for an explanation. But when no one showed, she took some clean clothes out of her suitcase and took a long, relaxing shower. It felt really good under the hot water and she reluctantly got out to dress. Kate glanced at the desk clock and saw she had about fifteen minutes until dinner – Nick would have reserved a large meeting room, or an extra room with a large sitting area, for their use as a place to hang out or eat. It was much easier to have the hotel staffs provide meals than try to go out in the city. The band had no trouble getting out and around but it was usually a nightmare for Nick. And, with a hotel this size, girls would be camping on the sidewalk in hopes of seeing someone famous; Nick definitely didn't have the patience to deal with it on a constant scale.

She stepped out of her room and one of the security people, Jake, pointed her in the direction of where everyone was. Dressed in what she would wear during the show, she pulled her damp hair up into a ponytail as she opened the door. Kate hesitated for a moment but everything seemed normal. She was hoping Brock hadn't said anything to Nick and this could just go away. The nervousness about it was leaving her stomach queasy, so she opted for half a sandwich off the tray and a bottle of water. She sat in a chair the furthest away from Nick as possible watching everyone to gauge the mood. Nothing seemed out of place as everyone was talking and eating as usual. Nick was deep in conversation with Mickey so Kate ate her sandwich quietly, relieved this might disappear with no fanfare. She definitely did not want her past events conflicting with this job.

When it was time to leave for the show, everyone got up and started heading out the door. Nick lagged back so he had to wait for Kate to pass him. As she got close, Nick's attention was focused on her. "We need to talk later," he said to her.

Kate sighed, knowing it would have been too easy for it to simply disappear. "I guess maybe we do. Please, do me a favor tonight, and I will explain it later?"

"Go ahead."

"When you introduce the band tonight, will you only introduce me as Kate? I have reasons for needing my last name left out and I will explain why later."

Nick nodded. "Stay close to us, love. Brock came back and said *he* is sitting in the lobby waiting for you to come back down." Kate knew he was talking about Kevin. "We have a diversion ready but you never know."

Kate was not happy he knew but she was impressed with his level of confidentiality. Nick could have brought the subject up in front of everyone and she was thankful he hadn't. It was a bad time in her life and having the nightmare resurface was doing nothing for her nerves. Kate kept focused, staying close to Trent because he was the tallest, next to Nick, and hoped she could blend in with him. She did not want another scene in the lobby, especially with Nick involved. As they got off the elevator, Kate could see security had Kevin's view obscured and she was already out the door and into a limousine before they moved. As soon as they saw the limo pull away from the curb, Nick's security people continued out the door. There were still two left on the hotel floor, to keep it secure, and there were two in each of the limousines.

Once at the Garden, Kate's nervousness started to ease up as she knew they had gotten away cleanly. She was now able to focus on the show and making sure she was ready. Kate had been afraid she was going to be so shaky it would have shown when she was playing some of the piano solos. She felt relieved her hands were no longer trembling. Kate noticed Brock was staying close by and she had no doubt Nick had instructed him to watch because he knew what Kevin looked like. Brock was imposing on his own – six-foot-six, two-hundred-fifty pounds and always looked like he was scowling. Kate knew it was part of his job persona – she had seen him laugh plenty of times on the bus.

The show went off without a hitch and security got them out of the building before the fans even knew they had left. It was all about timing, which is why Nick did interviews or fan events before the show. This made it much simpler to walk off the stage and straight into a waiting car. Kate's nerves were starting to make her stomach queasy again. She was not looking forward to telling this story to Nick, but knew that she didn't have much choice. If Kevin was going to be a problem, then Nick was going to have to make sure it didn't interrupt his schedule even if it meant being personally involved.

* * *

Because they had ridden on the bus the night before, once at the hotel, the rest of the band headed straight for their rooms and to their beds, instead of hanging out. Kate followed Nick as he walked toward the extra room they had. There was still hot coffee and Nick walked over, pouring them both a cup. Nick put sugar and cream in his and just a little sugar for Kate, clearly knowing how she preferred it. That was one of the many things he didn't miss about England; he much preferred American coffee over British tea. He set the cup down across the table from him and sat down, motioning for Kate to take the chair. She was being exceptionally quiet – Nick was certain she was a bundle of nerves about this.

"So, let's have the story. He's obviously someone you know, unless you go around slapping strange men in hotel lobbies," he started, trying to put a little levity in it to ease her nervousness.

Kate gave a little laugh. "No, it isn't one of my hobbies. His name is Kevin Miles and he's my ex-husband."

Nick's eyebrows rose, surprised, as if he wasn't expecting that relationship. "Ex-husband? You must have been a child when you married him."

"Not a child, but a dumb twenty-one." She paused for a moment. "How much of this do you really want, Nick?" she asked. "The bottom line is he insulted me as usual and I slapped him for being rude."

"I'm here for the long haul, love. Let's have the whole thing."

Kate took a deep breath and exhaled. "I met him at Julliard. We were juniors and we had a lot of the same classes. He was training for the same career – to be a concert pianist. He sat down across from me at a coffee shop one day and started being friendly." She took a sip of the coffee. "I was pretty naïve at twenty-one; I hadn't dated much in high school and had never had sex. So when he started paying attention to me, it went to my head. It was like one of those chick flicks, where everyone lives in a happy world - walks through the village, kissing on street corners, that kind of thing. But I think it frustrated him some I wouldn't sleep with him. I figured if I had waited this long, I might as well take it with me to my wedding bed. Naïve, I know."

"Honorable, but rare," Nick agreed. "Girls are getting pregnant in high school now. The whole taboo about sex is gone."

"So just before school let out in May, he proposed. Still being in what I thought was love with the guy, I accepted and we were married just after Memorial Day. And the summer was good. We took summer classes together, walked around Central Park, and enjoyed each day with the other. Then senior year classes started in the fall. This meant more on-hands piano classes and more chances for being seen by the concert industry. This is when Kevin started to change. The time we used to spend together at lunch or traveling to school was gone. When we were together at home, the smallest things would set him off into a fury of anger. At first I thought he was seeing someone − I thought he was trying to make me angry enough to walk out.

"So, I had him followed, but he didn't go anywhere other than school. My detective found him at the piano almost every waking moment and definitely not with another woman. Christmas was a nightmare. We got in a big argument on Christmas Eve and I went to midnight mass alone at St. Joseph's. I'm not Catholic but I was looking for the serenity to figure out what was going wrong. When I got back, he was sound asleep and we didn't talk all day on Christmas. I took the tree down in the morning, just to be rid of the whole holiday feeling. And it seemed to get worse after the New Year.

"In March, we both entered a contest. It was based on grades and an audition with the folks from the London Philharmonic. The prize was an internship of sorts; they paid all your expenses for two years in London and you got to play with them as they helped you come out as a featured pianist. Obviously it worked for Kevin, because, the last I heard, he's still with the London people."

"How were you going to handle a marriage across the ocean?" Nick asked. "In light of everything going on, I can't see where this would have been beneficial."

"I wasn't going to enter the contest. I was going to let him win, if he could, and we could make decisions if he won. I was in love enough that I'd have been willing to put my career on hold for his. But one of the arguments we got into when the notice to apply went out included his comments about how sloppy I was and how I was only going to be a minor musician. Those stung so I entered the contest out of spite. I knew my marriage was about over – I thought this would be a good way to make a new start and I began talking to an attorney about getting papers drawn up. I had the money to move out but something was keeping me there. Some kind of mental thought we could still work things out.

"The day before the audition, we got into a fight because I didn't go to the dry cleaners and pick up his shirts. He never asked me to go and I had no idea he had dropped any off in the first place. To get out of his way and defuse the situation, I walked out of the bedroom. He ran out of the room and pushed me down the stairs. We had a townhouse apartment and there were about twelve stairs from top to bottom. I passed out for a minute when I hit the floor and I awoke with my left arm dangling at a strange angle. Kevin walked up to me and I remember his words like they were yesterday, *'This should take care of the problem'*, and he took the heel of his boot and slammed it onto my left hand. I remember screaming before I blacked out."

Nick had a look of utter horror on his face. "You're telling me he did this on purpose?" He could feel the anger starting to well up inside. This was an odd emotion for Nick as he worked at not letting things get him visibly angry, especially where a woman was involved.

Kate nodded in assent. "Yes, but the police never saw it that way. After I woke up and called nine-one-one, an ambulance and the police came to the house. I gave them my testimony before I blacked out again as the paramedics were immobilizing my hand and my arm. I woke up next in the hospital emergency room, with a whole group of doctors talking about what to do next. The police arrested Kevin but they let him go after talking to him. The charges were dropped because he had no history of domestic violence and he managed to convince them I fell accidentally and the concussion I received was making me say things which weren't true, although I have no clue how I could have shattered my hand falling down the stairs.

"The doctors eventually decided to transfer me to Johns Hopkins in Baltimore, where they set my arm and did the first of three operations on my hand to try to repair the damage. The break in my arm was textbook, nice and clean. My hand was shattered in four places and it was touch and go for a while – the doctors weren't sure I would even get the use of it back. Three operations, six months of rehabilitation and I was able to clench it into a fist. It took me another year of absolute stubbornness to be able to play the piano again." She showed him the faint scars which crisscrossed her left hand.

"So what was Kevin doing during all this?"

"I have no clue, except I knew he'd won the internship. I called the attorney I'd hired, explained I never wanted to see his face again, and told him to get me out of the marriage. My mother and stepfather rented me an apartment in Baltimore so I would have a place to stay while I was going through the treatment, rather than living in a hotel. I got a part time job while I was going through rehab teaching kids how to play the piano. I could teach with my limited range and it gave me a small sense of accomplishment to be able to pay at least part of my own way. Then, as soon as the divorce was final and my rehab was completed, my stepfather adopted me and I moved back to Los Angeles. My own father died when I was fourteen, so there was no one to object. The idea was I wanted to drop out of view from what I knew in New York. There is no age limit for adoption even though I was twenty-four. That gave me my stepfather's last name, Thomas, so I would have a new name and a new life. Kevin has no idea I changed my name except to drop his. My maiden name was Williams; it's probably who he's been looking for.

"My stepfather, Allen, is a corporate lawyer and Michael Grayson is one of his golfing buddies. When I thought I could do something with my music, Allen called Michael up and asked him if he would audition me for studio work. There's always plenty of it going around and Allen thought it would be good for me to do something productive, as well as lucrative, with my music since my dream of being a concert pianist was gone. Michael was a lot like you during the audition. He knew I was over qualified but also didn't want my talents go somewhere else. I started working for him six years ago and you know the rest. I thought maybe Kevin would be civil, his voice sounded nice when he called my name. I should have known better; he was still the same Kevin. This is his normal behavior – he was pretending he was someone else before we got married. Like I said – young, dumb, and naïve."

Nick stood up, taking their coffee cups over to the tray on the table so the maids could pick them up when they came through to clean in the morning. "I'm not sure what to say, love," Nick started.

"Wasn't quite the story I was thinking I would get. We can keep him away from you while we're here, that's not an issue. I hire this security company because they are good at making me invisible from the public and we can do the same for you. You simply have to be willing to do what you are told and not do dumb things like sneak out or other such juvenile behavior."

"I won't," she confirmed. "I was afraid you would fire me, actually. The fact you are willing to help me is a surprise."

Nick spun slowly around to look at her. "I'm not going to fire you, Kate. This kind of stuff happens a lot, only it's usually with me."

Kate started to laugh. The relief of telling someone the whole sordid story made her feel relaxed and happy. "Thanks. I feel much better."

"You're welcome," he said. "I am heading off to bed. We can talk more tomorrow."

They both reached the door at the same time. Nick went to open it for her but paused for a moment, looking at her. At the exact moment, she looked at him - a litany of unspoken words crossed between them. Without hesitating, Nick moved closer and his lips brushed hers. The kiss was soft, almost asking a question. When they broke apart, Kate smiled at him, but didn't say anything as she slipped passed him and went to her room.

CHAPTER THREE

The next morning, as soon as he knew she would be in the office, Nick made a phone call to his secretary in California. He wanted the phone number for the chief executive at the Philharmonic in London – Nick was not going to leave Kate's ex-husband loose where he could terrorize her for the next two days. Terry, his secretary, said she would get it and call him back. Nick also had Sam find Brock and brought him in to talk. Brock nodded his head in assent when Nick instructed him to stay on Kate like glue. He knew what the ex-husband looked like and could keep Kate safe from what appeared to be a real nut job.

Terry called back about twenty minutes later with all the information Nick needed. The man's name was Arthur Glademan. Nick didn't know him but figured he wouldn't have an issue getting through to talk to him. And Nick was correct – Glademan's secretary put Nick through immediately and they proceeded to have a short, clipped conversation. Glademan admitted they had some problems with Kevin in the past. He tended to have issues with photographers and had been in some scrapes with the law. Nick outlined what had happened the night before in New York and made it clear he wanted him to pull Kevin back to London. Glademan only had to look at the top money sponsors for the symphony to know Nick was on that list and if he wanted him to stay on it, he would comply. He told Nick he would get Kevin on the first flight back.

Brock reported back after an hour; Kevin had gotten into a taxi and the doorman who hailed it told him he was headed for the airport. Nick was hoping this would be the end of it for Kate. What he really wanted to do was go have a nice talk with the man which ended up with him bloody on the floor, but Nick knew better than that. All his talk about staying out of the press would go down the drain if he was arrested for assault. It didn't stop him from thinking about how nice it would have felt, though. Kate's story from the night before gnawed at him. Nick was one of those people who could be really angry and it not show, but this would have taxed all of his patience – this kind of energy would take away from his music. Like he told Kate, this kind of stuff usually happened with him. It wasn't unusual for some fans to be a little crazed, physically wanting to take a piece of him home. This was why he had around the clock security when he was on tour. And he was angry at himself for letting those protective feelings in – Nick hadn't had any kind of a physical relationship with a woman in over eight years. He had been willing to concede to himself he was fine the way he was and a woman would only be trouble in his life. He had no idea why he kissed her.

The next six weeks were uneventful. The shows flowed as normal, with no issues with equipment, venue or people. They were about seven weeks from finishing when Nick got a phone call early one morning from his mother. She was crying and he was able to determine his father had passed away earlier in the morning. His mom, Tessa, was crying, begging him to come home to say his goodbyes. Nick calmed her down and promised he would get on the first flight to London. Once he hung up, he sat down on the bed and smoked a cigarette before calling Mickey's cell phone. It was only three in the morning, which was nine am, London time. Nick told Mickey he was going to have to cancel the remaining two shows during the week and almost all the stuff for the weekend, getting him back on Saturday so they could do the show Sunday night in Chicago. Mickey had been asleep but was wide awake as Nick explained the situation to him. Mickey, having been with Nick for over twenty years as his manager, knew the last thing Nick wanted to do was go anywhere near his family. A funeral was going to make it even worse. Mickey got a private jet for Nick and Sam, one of the two security agents who normally guarded Nick, and they were off from the local airport in Louisville, Kentucky. They would have a connection in New York – first class on a commercial airline and Nick wasn't looking forward to it either. The whole situation was leaving him with a sour feeling because he knew things would be strained between him and his brothers; if it hadn't been for his mother begging him on the phone, he wouldn't have gone. Mickey assured him he would take care of the band and get them to Chicago in time.

When the band members were assembled for breakfast, Mickey came and delivered the bad news, informing them Nick had left earlier with Sam for London. Everyone was saddened by Nick's loss and no one spoke much at breakfast. Mickey outlined the game plan – he was going to try to get them hotel rooms early in Chicago, so they could just go straight there, but if none were available they might have to stay in St. Louis for the weekend as previously planned. Once he was finished speaking, he walked over to Kate and silently handed her an envelope which was on hotel stationery. She slipped it into her back pocket, without reading it, and continued breakfast with the rest of the guys. Andy was telling everyone what he knew about Nick's family and to Kate it sounded depressing. And to have a funeral in the middle of such strife, she knew Nick was going to be walking into a virtual hornets nest. Nick was usually pretty good at handling stress but Kate wasn't sure about this situation.

After breakfast, she went back to her room and pulled the envelope out of her pocket. There was nothing on the front and Kate gently opened the seal, so as not to rip it, and pulled out the single sheet of paper. On it was a note in Nick's handwriting:

Kate,

Please call me tonight, around seven your time.

Nick

That was it – nothing about what he wanted her to do. Calculating the difference in time, it would be after midnight when she called. This told her he wanted her to call pretty much after the day's chaos was over. It struck her as odd he would leave her such a note – she thought he would have kept in touch with Mickey, since he was his manager. But, being as he was the boss, she had every intention of calling him as instructed. She was a little unsure about how she felt about Nick. He was her employer and she still saw him that way, but the occasional light kisses were starting to play on her imagination. Ever since New York, there had been a few solitary times when they were alone and it was starting to not be unusual for him to give her a friendly hug or a soft kiss. Was he really interested in her? Or was she just imaging things?

* * *

Nick arrived in London at eight pm, London time and there was a car waiting at the airport for him and Sam. Nick gave the driver the address to his parent's house in Islington. His head was pounding – he was dreading this worse than anything else in his life. He had the driver stay once he arrived because he was not spending the night there – Mickey had set up a hotel which was quiet and close to the house. His mom wasted no time wrapping her arms around him, crying, and wouldn't let go once he came into the house. It had been over five years since he had been home last and that visit had been in and out, so fans didn't realize he was there. The air was thick with disapproval as Nick looked over her shoulder at his eldest brother, Phillip. It was like looking into the mirror twenty years in the future, because there was a strong resemblance, but Phillip looked every one of his sixty-two years. Nick stayed guarded, not leaving any emotion open which Phillip could take advantage of. Instead he remained calm, a determined look on his face.

After soothing his mom, and assuring her he would be back in the morning, Nick and Sam got in the car, heading to the hotel. It was about ten minutes away and Mickey put the reservation in Sam's name to help keep things quiet. Nick told Sam he was going to bed and would see him in the morning. His headache was still there and he wasn't even interested in eating anything. Sam didn't say anything and gripped Nick's shoulder as he went into his room. The rooms were adjoining and Nick unlocked his side once he got in. He saw Sam do the same and they left the two doors open. Nick opened the curtains to the window and stared down at the city, trying to let his nerves settle down enough to even try to sleep. When he was stressed, Nick found that sometimes staring down at the city lights, as the busy cities were winding down to sleep, helped him relax. And he hated London – which was only making this worse.

His ringing cell phone brought him back to reality and he saw it was Kate. He smiled as he recognized the phone number, grateful she had gotten the message and called.

"Marshall."

"Nick, it's Kate," she said softly. "How are you doing?"

"I have a bloody headache," he answered honestly. "I've had it all day and it's only getting worse."

"Have Sam go down to the gift shop and get you something for it."

"It's all right, love. I'll probably have it non-stop the next three days anyway," Nick answered. "I'd only end up downing the whole bottle before it's all done. How are things there?"

"Mickey was able to change reservations so we're heading for Chicago in the morning. The plan is to hang out and wait for you to get back. Is there anything I can do for you?"

"You're doing it. I just wanted to talk to you. Hear a friendly voice."

"I'm here for you, Nick," she replied quietly. "The phone works both ways."

"I know… and I might call you if things get any worse than they already are."

"How's your mom doing?"

"She's a wreck," he said. "She wrapped her arms around me, crying, and wouldn't let go. That almost started a fight with Phillip and I."

"She's glad to see you. And she's hurting from the loss of your dad," Kate said.

"I know, love, I know. I just can't wait until Trevor shows up. Then the two of them can gang up on me." Nick answered in a sarcastic tone. "Phillip by himself is trouble enough. Together they take sides and I am usually on the receiving end of their rants.

"Nick," she said, chiding him gently. "Use that whole impatient-angry tone you've perfected. It should definitely back them off."

Nick started to laugh. "Are you implying I use that tone a bit?"

"When you're frustrated, yes," she confirmed. "Reminds me of my dad when he would get angry. You suddenly have the need to go find somewhere else to be."

Nick couldn't stop laughing. "Thanks, love. I really needed a laugh."

"No charge. Now go to bed and try to keep calm. You have a long day ahead."

"Yes, ma'am," he answered. "Call me again later this evening? Seven your time?"

"I'll call. Night, Nick."

"Night."

Nick felt so much better after the call with Kate. And, unless his senses were off because of the headache, he heard a lot more in Kate's voice than a worried employee. Or even a concerned friend. This would be something to investigate when he got back, although he was still not sure how he felt about her. He liked her – he liked her a lot, actually, but those kinds of feelings in him had been dead since his divorce. He had tried to resurrect them in his previous relationships but he felt like he was only going through the motions. The feelings had stayed dead, leaving him to enjoy their company but there were no solid connections. Even in bed, he felt detached. After hearing Kate's ordeal, though, he wanted to be there for her and protect her. And him wanting to do something major to the ex-husband wasn't normally Nick's style.

The next two days were nothing short of a headache-inducing terror for Nick. Over and over he tried to exercise control so he wouldn't say what he really felt about his brothers, trying to not upset his mum. Word leaked out Nick was there and, before anyone knew what was happening, there was a small crowd of young girls and a couple of reporters for some tabloid magazines in front of the house. This started the first argument with Phillip over how he brings trouble with him. Before it escalated into a brawl with him, Nick called the London studio and got some of the public relations guys out with pictures and things for a distraction, clearing everyone out. The reporters were harder because they only went as far as their cars – they were going to get pictures and a story no matter what. The two got in each other's faces but at least no punches were thrown and Sam did his best to back Nick off. The arguing made his mom cry more and they were both apologizing to her, but not to each other. For Nick, the gloves were off. All he looked forward to each day was the call from Kate at night. She had a way of calming his nerves and helping to make his headache recede.

The funeral was graveside. All the family got into waiting cars from the funeral home and went out to the cemetery. There was no formal service inside the chapel, but a funeral carriage was led out from within the main chapel – the wrap-around windows on the carriage showed the casket inside. Four majestic white horses led the carriage to the cemetery. The family, then friends, walked behind it to the gravesite. Nick was good with no other service; he had plans to be on a plane back to the States as soon as it was over. The service was solemn and lasted about an hour, after which everyone went back to the house. Phillip's wife, Catherine, picked up the two suitcases which were by the door and rushed Tessa out of the house. The plans were for her to spend some time in Leeds with Phillip's family, until she got her bearings again. Tessa said goodbye to Nick before following her daughter-in-law out to their car. As soon as Tessa was outside, Phillip and Trevor forcefully shoved Nick up against a wall in the living room.

"Get out of here, Nick," Phillip said through clenched teeth. "And don't plan on coming back."

"What the hell is your bloody problem?" Nick answered, pushing them both off him. "Last time I checked, she was my mum too."

"She doesn't need the chaos which follows you everywhere. Dad never approved and we don't either."

"That's not true," Nick said defending himself and brushing out his shirt sleeves. "Dad and I came to an understanding years ago." His dad hadn't been excited about his choice of career, but had grudgingly given in he had been very successful at it. More so than he had ever thought Nick would be. "It wasn't exactly what he'd wanted but he admitted I had done well and even said I made him proud."

Sam walked into the house and reviewed the scene. "Nick, the car is here," he said, his voice making it clear he didn't like whatever had transpired.

"Just remember what I said, Nick," Phillip said. "We don't want you back."

Phillip and Trevor walked away and Nick leaned back against the wall. "What was that about?" Sam asked.

"Doesn't matter, mate," Nick said in a defeated voice. "Let's get the hell out of here."

Nick was quiet as they drove to the hotel to get their bags. At the hotel, his resolve started to break. His hands were shaking as he lit a cigarette and sat down on the bed, trying to calm his nerves. He could hear Sam telling him they needed to go so they could catch their flight, but his mind was blocking out everything except what happened with Phillip and Trevor. Nick knew the crowds which tended to find him were annoying, but he could not comprehend what made the two of them dislike him so much. His brothers were so much older; by the time Nick had gotten to primary school they were already in college. Phillip had a son who wasn't much younger than Nick. They had never been close.

Nick was startled back to reality as Sam pulled him up off the bed and started pushing him toward the door. Sam was telling him they would miss their plane if he didn't get moving and he allowed Sam to lead him to the car. Nick was quiet in the backseat on the ride to the airport and during the flight to New York for the connection to Chicago. Sam tried to talk to him, but Nick wasn't interested in idle conversation. Finally, in the first class lounge at La Guardia, in New York, Nick spoke, answering Sam when he asked about the status of his headache.

"I still have it mate," Nick answered.

"I can go get some aspirin from one of the shops," Sam offered.

Nick shook his head. "I'm fine."

"Want to tell me what happened at your mom's house before we left?" Sam asked.

Nick's expression was hard. "It's not important," he said finally. "Let it go."

Nick was quiet but there was a definite quality in his tone, letting Sam know Nick was not interested in discussing it. There was no more conversation between them. Nick went back to his thoughts, still trying to hash out in his mind what brought on the events at the house.

Nick arrived in Chicago around dinner time but didn't go into the room with the band, opting to shut himself up in his. He immediately sent Jake to get a bottle of Scotch and a glass. Once satisfied, Nick gave Sam specific instructions; he wanted to be alone the rest of the evening and, unless something caught fire or a natural disaster occurred, he didn't want any interruptions.

CHAPTER FOUR

The band was headed to Steve's room to play poker and the guys tried to talk Kate into going with them. She turned them down, saying she had a headache and was going to watch some television or read a book. After they took off, Kate instead decided to go talk to Nick. His phone conversation last night led her to believe things had continued to be horrible and she wanted to help with any residual effects this was having. She had lost her dad while in high school and knew how grief felt, and how it took its toll on people. Based on what Andy had been saying, she knew Nick had other baggage associated with his parents and his brothers, too.

She knocked on the suite door and Sam answered it. He let her into the sitting room, but warned her - Nick was in a bad mood, said not to disturb him and he probably wouldn't talk to her. Sam appeared to be bothered by Nick's mood, which Kate interpreted as he was willing to take the hit for not following orders; otherwise he would have turned her away at the door. *What was the worst he could do?* Kate thought. *Throw me out? Fire me?*

Kate knocked on the door leading to Nick's bedroom. "Better be bloody important," was the answer she heard.

Kate mentally counted to ten, then opened the door. She went inside, quietly closing it behind her. Inside she saw his suitcase along the wall and found Nick standing in front of the large picture window, staring down at the city lights. There was a half empty bottle of Scotch on the table next to him and he didn't turn around as she stepped further into the dimly lit room. Kate didn't say anything as she walked up behind him, putting her arms around his waist. Nick stiffened in reply at the foreign touch but after a few minutes, she felt him start to relax against her. She remained quiet, wanting him to get comfortable with her there. There was no doubt in her mind how she felt about him, boss or otherwise, and she was not going to let him drown himself in this pain, whatever had transpired. She was sensing something more than just the funeral, which was depressing enough on its own. No, something happened and it was tearing him up. She had never seen him drink alcohol straight before. Matter of fact, she rarely saw him drink anything alcoholic in the almost six months they had toured together. The rest of the band drank their share of beer and other drinks, but Nick was almost never with them. And then only a single glass of something.

"Was it bad?" she asked softly, finally deciding to break the silence. The fact he hadn't instantly tossed her out, Kate took as a positive sign.

"It was bad," he confirmed, continuing to stare out the window and drink the Scotch he was holding.

He showed no intention of moving out of Kate's embrace and rested against her. "This is why I have American citizenship, so I don't have to go back to England. And, after this European tour, love, if I even remotely talk about doing anything in London, I want you to lock me up somewhere in a mental ward."

This confirmed to Kate something had happened outside of the onerous tasks of making the arrangements for a funeral. She stood behind him, idly rubbing his shoulders and leaning her head on his back. She was letting him do all the talking – let him talk the pain out. "The hell of it was my mum was glad for me to be there," he continued, finishing the Scotch and pouring more into the empty glass. "The rest was a stark lesson in patience as I tried to keep my feelings to myself. Not always successfully, I might add."

She hugged him tighter. "I'm sorry."

"And it didn't help when the press showed up at the house. British tabloids are much more aggressive than they are here in the States. I had to get one of the London PR guys to come clear them out; it only added more fuel to the fire. And, trust me, it was a roaring bonfire by the time we got to the funeral."

She could feel him shake, sensing tears had started. Kate was content to hold him, letting him work it out, waiting for him to tell her what went so wrong. "I was born later in my parent's life," he volunteered. "My parents had waited until they were in their thirties to have kids so they were almost fifty when I came along. They had thought they were done having kids with my brothers and then here I came. And my dad all but disowned me when I was a teenager. He thought my music was frivolous and was adamant I needed to go to school to learn some kind of a respectable trade. Both my brothers had already finished college long before and had careers; Phillip is a banker and Trevor is a professor at Oxford."

"They're a lot older than you?" Kate asked.

"Trevor is the closest but there are more than fourteen years between us," Nick answered. "Even after I had success and became what I am, my dad was a long time in forgiving. And he passed his disapproval to both of my brothers." Nick was silent and Kate didn't push him. She merely held him against her, waiting for him to go on with the story. She suspected he was getting close to what had happened.

"After the funeral, we went back to my mum's house. I barely had time to say goodbye to her as she was leaving to stay with Phillip and his family in Leeds for a while. Once she was in the car with his family, both Phillip and Trevor backed me against a wall, told me to get the hell out of the house, and not to come back."

Oh my god, Kate thought. *What do you even say to that?* Kate silently watched him pour more Scotch in the glass and, before picking it up, he broke out of the embrace, turning to face her. She saw the remnants of his tears and gently reached up, wiping away the rest. His mouth found hers in a kiss — not the soft gentle ones they had been sharing previously — but an assault on her mouth with his tongue. He scared her at first as he held her face in his hands, but she remained calm, knowing it was the stress driving him to be so fierce.

When Nick lifted his head, he pulled her to him in a tight embrace. "I didn't mean to be so rough, love," he said softly. "You should probably get out of here before you end up in that bed."

"I'm not leaving until I'm sure you're okay," she countered.

Nick gave her another hug before releasing her. "I'm good. Thanks to you," he answered. "And thank you for the phone calls. They were a lifesaver."

"I suspected you had a reason for giving Mickey the message for me. It was an odd request."

"I needed a lifeline. I debated about even going when my mum called because I knew there would be trouble." Nick ran his fingers through his hair which was now flowing down his back. He usually pulled it back in a ponytail during the day unless he was onstage. He smiled down at her. "I didn't quite expect what happened. But it's all right."

"Then I'll go," Kate said quietly. She stepped closer to him and pulled his head down to hers to finish the kiss. His arms came around her holding her to him. He eventually pulled away and turned back to the window.

"Now you really better get out of here," he growled at her.

Kate touched him one more time then went out the door. She talked a minute with Sam who confirmed what Kate had suspected –things with his oldest brother had been exceptionally bad. Sam asked if Nick had told her what had happened before they left and she skirted at the details, saying they had said some hurtful things, but not wanting to tell Nick's secrets. She also mentioned the Scotch and suggested he get some food brought up, otherwise Nick wouldn't be in any shape to do a show tomorrow night. An entire bottle of the Scotch was just asking for a hangover.

* * *

The next morning around nine, the band was eating breakfast when Nick strode into the room. He walked over and got a cup of coffee then laid the sheet music he had brought with him next to Kate on the table. Kate glanced at the title *'Winning it All'*. Nick turned the chair around backwards and sat down next to her.

There was nothing from last night to indicate Nick had ever been upset. He also gave no hint about their kiss or what emotion was going through him at this moment looking at Kate. Nick knew he wanted her, although the argument she worked for him continued to keep him level. But the veneer was cracking. And as much as he wanted to deny it to himself, Nick knew he was falling hard for her.

"Would you have time today to go through this music?" Nick asked her.

Kate picked up the stack and thumbed through it. "I suppose I can get a car and go out to the arena to run it. What is it?"

"It's the opening theme for the next James Bond movie," he said.

"Seriously?" Kate asked surprised. "Since when do you have time to write movie music?"

"What the hell do you think I do at night while you guys are all out carousing the bars?" he asked. "Play tiddly-winks?"

"Normal people sleep," Kate said as the rest of the guys burst into laughter.

"There's the problem, Kate," Dave interrupted. "Nick's not normal. He's a machine."

"Laugh it up, mate," Nick said good-naturedly. "We have about two days when we get back to record this song. Everything."

Dave rolled his eyes. "Sometimes working for you is no picnic."

Nick continued to smile at them. "So, if the piano piece works, I have the rest of the music ready and we can start rehearsing it before we get back. I don't like doing my own arranging and I really hate writing piano music, so I need you to run through it. Make sure it's fluid."

Kate was playing it in her head and almost didn't hear what Nick was saying. "Sure, Nick," she said finally. "I'll get one of the security guys to get me a car out there this morning."

* * *

Kate left the room and found Brock outside the elevator talking with Jake and Kyle, two of the other security people. There were eight security guys total - Sam and Mike, who were Nick's main security, Brock, who had unofficially become hers after the events in New York, Jake, Kyle, Ryan, Tim, and Jason. She asked Brock if he would get her a car to the arena, showing him the stack of sheet music Nick had given her. He agreed without hesitation and she went to her room, getting a few things before leaving. Kate had long since given up taking a purse anywhere. First, she never needed it since Nick paid for just about everything, including their entertainment, like the trips to the pubs and bars. Second, it was something else to keep track of. She put a couple of dollars in her pocket so she could buy a bottle of water if she wanted at the arena, and grabbed the half empty one on the table from last night. Making sure she had her room key in her back pocket, she stepped out into the hallway and Brock motioned for her to follow him.

The limo dropped them off at the arena where the show was tonight. Kate had told Brock he didn't have to hang around but her suggestion went nowhere. Nick had hired him to protect his band members and protect was what he was going to do. Kate walked up on the stage and sat down at the piano. In the beginning, she'd wondered why Nick went through the hassle of dragging a piano around but now she considered it a godsend. She put the music on the stand, lifted the keyboard cover, and started reading through the music. Kate had endured many classical pieces since learning to play but some of these music measures were a little intimidating. She went through the song a couple of times and asked Brock if he could go find her something to write with. About midway through the song, it started feeling hesitant. Kate's thought was she'd make the correction notes and take it back to Nick for his input. Songwriting was not her specialty, but she had been taught the basics of how to write music when she was at Julliard. Brock found a pencil for her and Kate was lost again in the music.

* * *

About two hours later, Nick came strolling onto the stage with her. He stopped for a moment and watched her while she was deep in thought. *This was why I wanted a piano player and not someone who could just play keyboards*, Nick thought. It looked like she was making notes and, once he got closer to her, he saw she was writing new music notes. "Find something you didn't like, love?" Nick asked.

Kate jumped as he spoke; she hadn't heard him walk across the stage. "It sounds wrong through the middle. I was making some notes on how to possibly correct it."

"I didn't know you wrote music," he said, surprised.

Kate shook her head. "I don't as a rule. But I know the basics and this section is choppy. I was going to bring it back so you could review it."

"Why don't we go through it now? That's why I came over. Run through the melody and we could see if what I had put together worked."

"Sounds good to me. It's nice, from what I've been playing. I was trying to picture it with the rest of the guitars and Trent stomping with his lead foot on the bass drum."

Nick laughed and pulled out the acoustic guitar he always kept with him, rather than transporting it on the truck with the rest of the gear. It wasn't bright and shiny like the electric one he usually played on stage. This one was much older and showed obvious use. Pulling up the drummer's stool, he sat down next to Kate. He counted off three and Kate started to play. It was a good minute before he started. When they got to the part Kate had been working on, she stopped. Nick stopped with her, lifting his eyebrows to question her.

"Which version do you want? Yours or mine?"

"Let go with yours. I know what mine sounded like, love," he answered.

They went back to the start of the verse and Nick could easily hear the changes she had made. And they seemed to fit nicely. This suited him fine because he hated doing arrangements. The studio had a company they contracted with to do this kind of work, but the movie guys had called before he flew to London, informing him the release of the movie had been moved up. They needed the title song in seven weeks – which was the week they got back to Los Angeles, in between the two tours.

"Rock on," he told her. "I like what you did. "

"Me too," she agreed.

"We don't have time to mess with it. I need to have the song done in six weeks. Everything – all the parts - and it has to be perfect the first time around because we won't have a week to make corrections."

"Why the push?" Kate asked.

"The movie producers changed the movie release date to spring break," he answered. He continued to play a couple of cords and strum a few notes. "Last night," he said, a mischievous smile turning up the corners of his mouth. "Sam wasn't supposed to let anyone in the room."

"I got that part," Kate said. "Your greeting wasn't exactly blooming with sunshine."

"I should be angry about it. I gave him pretty direct orders," Nick said, in a definite tone. "They don't usually disobey direct orders."

"So why aren't you angry then?"

"Because all my anger went out the window with your touch," Nick told her softly. "I lost this argument with myself last night; I need to know how you feel, love. Because I'm not going to open myself any further if this road is going nowhere."

"I like you, Nick," Kate answered him honestly, her tone level and smooth. "More than just a friend or my boss. I almost couldn't stand the calls from London – all I could hear was the hurt in your voice and I was powerless to help."

"You did more than you know," Nick confirmed. "But let me ask you this – do you have the patience to wait another six weeks to sort this out? Right now I'm your boss and it's the difficulty I'm having. I've already said and done more than I should."

"What's going to be different in six weeks? I'll still work for you," Kate said. "Unless you plan to fire me when we get back."

Nick smiled at her. "I'm not going to fire you, Kate. But I barely know you – outside of the fact you like sugar in your coffee and don't like to leave your hair down."

"It gets in the way when I play," Kate said, amusement sparkling in her eyes as she teased him.

"Good to know, love," he said, laughing as he put the guitar back in the case. "Seriously though, are you game for this? I'll tell you straight up I'm a difficult bastard most of the time."

"I know, Nick. But it's only a mask you put on so people don't get close."

"Letting people close only gets you hurt," Nick answered quietly. "That's why the way I feel about you is scaring the hell out of me. But I don't want to spend any more time guessing whether you feel the same."

"I can handle six weeks," Kate said, looking at him intently.

Nick smiled broadly at her. "Ready to go back to the hotel?" He asked, standing up. He held a hand down to her and she stood up beside him.

Nick released her hand, picked up the guitar, and started down the stairs with Kate beside him. They walked over to where Brock and Mike were waiting. "You weren't serious, were you," Kate asked, "about this is all you do at night?"

Nick laughed, liking how she moved back into a generic conversation. "No, I was giving you all crap," he admitted. "I've been spending a lot of time writing this song, but I spend most of my free time on the phone with the studio."

"Checking up on you?"

"Not exactly," Nick said. "I own half of it. I have lots of work to do there which has nothing to do with my music. Recording my own records and going out on the road, that's what I do for fun."

"Wow," Kate exclaimed. "I didn't know you had so many irons in the fire."

"Keeps me busy, love," he answered. "I do less thinking."

Nick didn't have to say any more. He was glad they had this conversation; he had been a little nervous starting it, for fear she was going to reject him. And he was going to have to figure out how to get past the block he had as her boss if this was going to work. But he was really pleased she was willing to be patient with the whole mechanics of this odd relationship. Women in his past experience wanted his attention full time and were not patient about anything. This was a refreshing change for him and one of the things he liked about her.

CHAPTER FIVE

The next few weeks were smooth – everyone could feel the end of the tour looming and it was easy to see everyone was ready to have some time away. All the band members got along; it's just hard to have the same people day in and day out in your face. Nick was making a subtle effort toward Kate, which didn't escape her notice. Simple things like ending up next to her at dinner, being in the same limousine to each venue, or joining the almost-nightly poker game, she saw as him trying to spend more time with her. Kate asked Andy about it one night, wanting to make sure his behavior wasn't unusual, and he told her Nick tended to be a lot more relaxed in the last shows. Andy's opinion was there wasn't as much chaos with only two or three weeks until the end.

The final city of the US tour was in Monterey, California, and Kate wasn't her usual energetic self. During the last two shows she was less outspoken, and tonight, she wasn't saying much to anyone. Tomorrow they would be back in Los Angeles and the following day, Monday, they would be in the studio recording the song for the movie. Kate knew she was sick but was doing her best to keep it from the others and especially Nick. The fever wasn't too bad but her throat was sore. She was glad she didn't sing because tonight there would be no chance. Her voice was giving out – it was raspy now and she kept quiet to hide it. Hot tea, which was soothing, helped with the disguise. After the show, champagne came out and everyone was celebrating in the dressing room. When the others were well into the festivities, she pulled Brock away and asked him to get her a car back to the hotel. Brock questioned why she wanted to leave early and she was as straight as she could be, telling him she had a headache and didn't feel good. It wasn't a lie but the achiness was starting to drag her down. Lucky for her he complied, getting her into a limo and traveled with her as was normal. Kate went straight up to the fifth floor and into her room, putting on her lounging pajamas – the ones she normally wore before she went to bed. Kate slept naked as a normal rule, but she was chilled to the bone and wanted as much warmth as possible. She made another cup of tea with the hot water portion of the small coffee maker in her room and settled into the pillows watching a little television. No one had noticed she had left early.

The ride back to Los Angeles was going to be about five hours. The tea she had been drinking, almost by the gallon, had restored her voice enough to sound almost normal. She told the others she hadn't slept well and was going to crash for part of the trip. No one questioned her and she asked Brock to wake her up when they got within an hour of Los Angeles. Brock agreed – she wasn't fooling him any and he knew she was sick. She knew he was fond of her and was willing to keep her secret as long as she didn't get any sicker than she was. If this happened, then she knew he would have to tell Nick. At least he could understand her wanting to keep things quiet and not get anyone else involved.

As instructed, Brock woke her up as they were passing though Santa Barbara, which was roughly an hour out. The nap had helped some, but Kate was aware she was going to have to stay focused to keep up the ruse. She stayed to the end of one couch, drinking a bottle of water and listening to the guys argue over which football team was the best. Since she wasn't a football fan, she was content to be a bystander and not participate. Looking toward the front of the bus, she saw Nick sitting up in the front seat across from Mickey. He smiled at her when their eyes met.

Before pulling into the studio parking lot, Nick reminded everyone to be at the studio in the morning by six so they would have the entire day to get the track done. Kate was thankful she would have today to sleep and possibly get on the other side of whatever this bug was. Putting her suitcases in the trunk of her car, she left for home without saying anything to anyone. Nick had gotten off the bus and gone inside the studio building with Mickey, so she had been able to sneak away quietly and without fanfare. The drive to her house was only about thirty minutes and Sunday traffic was light. Once inside her apartment, she turned the heater on because it was ice cold in the place. After making herself a comfortable nest on the couch, she fell asleep almost immediately.

* * *

She awoke to her cell phone ringing and the caller ID showed it was Nick. Kate thought about not answering it but knew he would get irritated if she didn't. "Hello?"

"Kate?" he asked his voice a little confused.

"It's me, Nick," she said, her voice raspy again while she slept.

There was a brief pause on the other end. "Why the hell didn't you tell me you were sick, love?"

Nice, she thought. *Now he's worked up about this*. "I didn't tell anyone," she said defending herself. "I didn't want anyone to worry over me. I'll be fine. I had a nap on the bus and have been sleeping since I got home. I feel better already."

"You don't sound *better*," Nick countered. "I'm coming over. What's your address?"

"Nick, you don't have to come all the way out here," she protested. "I'm fine, really."

There was another pause on the phone. "Kate, if I have to turn around and go back to the studio to look up your address, I'm not going to be a very happy person when I get there."

She sighed, knowing it was pointless to argue with him. "1818 Hastings Court. It's in Huntington Beach."

"Fabulous, I'm almost there. I live above you in Sunset Beach."

Fabulous was not the word Kate was thinking of. One never knew what Nick was going to be sensitive over. Steve had been sick about three weeks into the tour and Nick never said anything special to him about it. "You don't have to come over here," she tried again.

"Kate." That was all he said. Then as an afterthought, "I'll be there in fifteen minutes." And he disconnected their call.

Since all she had done since coming home was sleep, Kate took a minute to put her suitcases in the bedroom and made sure her hair wasn't standing straight up. She never liked being fussed over when she was sick – leave her alone and let it run its course. This was one of the negative perks of starting a relationship with a man who was used to things going his way. He was not going to be happy until everything was how he wanted it.

Almost fifteen minutes exactly, the doorbell rang and Kate got up to let Nick inside. She had seen this look on his face before but last time it hadn't been directed at her. She knew he was at the very least irritated. She watched him as he looked around her condo; she had floor to ceiling windows in the living room giving an excellent ocean view. She kept watching his expression as he took in the room, seeing it was starting to soften it some. She was not feeling well enough to deal with any of his hard moods.

"Nice place," he commented.

Kate went back to the couch and pulled the blanket over her. "You didn't have to come over here," she repeated, feeling like a broken record. Only this time, she got a stern look as Nick turned to face her.

"With anyone else, maybe," he answered. "But not you. I wanted to see for myself you were '*fine*' and you sure don't look it to me, love."

"I'll bet you don't look glamorous when you're sick," she retorted.

Nick started to laugh. "That's my Kate. Are you sure you'll be okay tomorrow?"

Kate nodded. "I'll be fine. Not like I have to sing any of it."

"True," he agreed, sitting down beside her on the couch. "Promise you will tell me next time? I almost had a heart attack when I heard your voice and realized I hadn't dialed a wrong number."

Kate laid her head on his shoulder. "I promise."

Nick put his arm around her. "You're running a fever," he said, concerned.

"I took some stuff for it after you called. Just have to let it run its course."

"Doesn't mean I have to like it, love," he replied, tightening his arms to hold her close.

* * *

By six the next morning everyone was gathered at the studio as scheduled. Kate didn't feel much better than she did the day before; however, the dizziness was gone. She was hoping this would all go well so they could get out early and she could go back home and sleep. Nick had promised her yesterday they would try to lay her stuff down first so she could get out as fast as possible. And, as usual, things did not go so smoothly at first and it was after two before they got something Nick was happy with. The sound room played it into the studio for everyone to listen to and there were a lot of high fives and people cheering. The rest of the band started to file out of the studio and as Kate stood up, the dizziness was back. She put a hand on the stool to steady herself and started to take a step when the world went black. She fell to the floor.

One of the sound guys yelled and the crowd came running back into the studio. Nick plowed his way to the front, trying to get to her. She was unconscious when he reached her and he scooped her up in his arms, taking her out into one of the waiting rooms where there was an overstuffed couch. Nick set her on it and tried to wake her up. Her eyes fluttered open and she went into a coughing fit as the panic of everyone there enveloped her. Nick motioned one of the public relations guys over and sent him up to his secretary to call the private doctor Nick used. If he wasn't available, Nick would take her to the emergency room at the hospital, but he preferred to avoid that. Someone brought over a glass of water and handed it to Nick.

"Drink this, love," Nick said, putting her hands around the cup. She took a small drink and handed the cup back to Nick. Kate started to get up and he pushed her back down. "Stay down, Kate. We have a doctor coming."

"Since when do doctors make house calls?" she asked hoarsely, in between coughs.

The PR guy came back and whispered something to him. "When you pay them enough," Nick answered her. Nick stood up and tossed everyone out of the room but himself and Kate. She had closed her eyes again and Nick reached out, touching her hand. He was rewarded with her opening her eyes, which told him she was still there. "It's okay, love," he said softly. "We'll get you looked at and then I'll take you home."

Kate nodded her assent and Nick left the room. He let the rest of the band know she was okay, telling them she had been sick for a couple of days. They were a family and the guys were visibly concerned about her. Nick said he had a doctor coming for a house call and they weren't surprised - they were used to Nick doing things most normal people didn't do. They left reluctantly; most had planned vacations with their families during the break. Nick assured them he would take care of Kate.

The private doctor, a longtime friend of Nick's partner, Jerry, came quickly. Nick liked that he was discreet and could be called out of the office. Nick tried to limit the amount of places he went and sitting in a doctor's office for what seemed like forever, was not high on his list. The doctor looked Kate over, listened to her heart, lungs, and looked at her throat. He was a little concerned she was running almost a one-hundred-four degree fever but Nick assured him he was going to take her home and get it down. The doctor said he thought she had strep throat and was certain she had fainted due to dehydration and not enough rest. He prescribed some medicines and Nick sent one of the studio runners – kids hired to do menial tasks - to go pick it up from the pharmacy down the street. While they waited, Nick took five minutes to go up to his office to grab his car keys and his wallet; he normally threw both in a desk drawer when he got there each day instead of carrying them around. Once the runner was back, he helped Kate to her feet and she seemed able to stand and walk with him. He helped her outside and into his car.

She was asleep before they got to the freeway and Nick drove silently to his house in Sunset Beach. There was no way he was going to leave her alone until she was over this. Once at his house, he picked her up off the seat and she stirred a little, but didn't wake up. Nick took her upstairs to one of the spare bedrooms; the house had five bedrooms as well as the master. He laid her on the bed and realized she couldn't sleep in the clothes she was wearing. Nick called for his housekeeper, Consuelo, to come help. She was an older lady from Puerto Rico he had hired over ten years ago. Consuelo shooed him out of the room and got one of his shirts from the closet for her to use as a nightshirt. She got her situated in the bed, then let Nick back in. Kate had never awoken during the process.

"Who is she, Señor Nick?" she asked, as they walked out of the room.

"She's my keyboard player," he answered. "She passed out on the studio floor and the doctor thinks she has strep. I brought her here to keep an eye on her."

"We will take care of her," Consuelo agreed.

Kate slept almost constantly for the next two days. She woke up long enough to take the pills the doctor prescribed and to eat a little of the soup Consuelo had prepared for her. Kate had panicked when she woke up in a strange bed, but Nick had been reading through contracts in a chair close by and was able to calm her down. He had not left the house in the two days she was there. It felt strange to him to be caring so much about another person. It was an emotion he had not felt in a long time. Not since he thought the child Sharon had borne was his, but this feeling was significantly different. On the third day, she felt well enough to take a shower and Kate said she felt a lot better afterwards. Nick wasn't allowing her out of bed for very long but he let her take a pillow and blanket onto the couch in the media room downstairs, so she could watch some television. She got settled comfortably and turned to look at Nick who had sat down on the coffee table across from her.

"You scared me big time, love," he started when their eyes met.

"I didn't mean to," she answered quietly. "All of a sudden, everything went black."

"Do you think you will be all right for a few hours here with Consuelo?" he asked. "I really need to go to the studio but I won't leave if you don't want me to."

Kate shook her head. "Go, Nick. Consuelo will help me if I need. "

Nick bent over and kissed her forehead. "I won't be long," he promised.

CHAPTER SIX

Kate was upstairs brushing her hair when Nick got home. She was sitting on the bed, counting each stroke as she pulled the brush through the long strands. Although she wore it up in a ponytail most of the time, it flowed in a red river down her back, almost to her hips. Nick stood in the doorway watching, drawn towards her and wanting to touch her hair. He finally came over, sitting next to her and she smiled at him. As he pulled a strand of her hair through his fingers, his lips softly touched hers. Kate returned the kiss and it started to go from a gentle kiss to something with a lot of hunger behind it. Nick pulled away first and stood up, moving to the window. Kate sat on the edge of the bed watching him.

"What happens if we cross that threshold, love?" he asked. "The first time I say something which angers you, are you going to walk out because now our relationship is personal and not just professional?"

"I haven't walked out yet, Nick," she answered. "And you have said lots in the past six months which angered me."

"Maybe, but that was boss to employee. Not lover to lover. Or," he hesitated, "husband to wife."

Kate's heart started beating a little faster. "Did you just propose marriage?"

"Kate," he started. "I love you. Watching you for the past three days has more than made it clear to me. I still have this crazy boss/employee hang up and being married would eliminate the problem."

"This is nuts," Kate countered. "I know the last thing you want to do is get married."

"You probably think I'm crazy."

Kate stood and went over to Nick. She was wearing one of his silk shirts and it was having an effect on Nick as she stood there. Kate put her hand on his chest. "I don't think you're crazy, Nick," she said softly. "I only know this."

Nick watched Kate stand on her tiptoes to kiss him. He growled as he picked her up and set her on the bed. He took a second to close the door and lock it, turning back to her as she was slowly unbuttoning the shirt. He watched as she finished and she pushed it off of her shoulders. Once completely naked, she got off the bed, walking over to him. She pulled his shirt loose from his pants and started to unbutton it. He watched her intently, devouring the sight of her and helped her finish with his clothes, leading her back to the bed. Sliding into bed, Nick pulled her on top of him.

Theirs was a time of loving and learning. Each touch, each kiss, learning everything about the other. Nick wanted to prolong it out, learn every inch of her, but his patience was limited. He had wanted this from her the first time he saw her but it was a feeling he had kept to himself; until the night she had told him about her ex. After New York, Nick still tried to stay away but he just couldn't stop himself. Those kinds of feelings had been dead since his divorce and he had been angry with himself in the beginning they were back. What happened in Chicago more than told him he needed Kate, and he wrestled with the fact she worked for him. To simply get her into bed was akin to a manager trying to bed his secretary. It didn't matter they both were not married; it was the principle of the idea. But after seeing her so sick, he knew he didn't want to lose her. And he knew he didn't want to be alone any more. This was the last thought in his mind as he surrendered himself to her.

* * *

They went downstairs and made sandwiches to eat. Consuelo had left after Nick returned home from the studio, so they had the kitchen to themselves. Kate assured Nick she was feeling well enough to come down with him and they had fun teasing each other as they ate the simple roast beef sandwiches. It was a feeling of 'home' Nick hadn't felt in a long time and he smiled at Kate, dressed in one of his shirts, since she only had one outfit there – the one she had been wearing in the studio on Monday. After dinner they went back to his bedroom. They made love again – more poignant and with less haste than the first time.

"Can I ask you something," Kate asked as she lay draped on Nick's chest.

"You can ask me anything, love," he answered.

Kate paused a few minutes, getting her words to together. She looked squarely into his eyes. "Nick, you are the most confident, outgoing, outspoken, organized person I have ever met. Everything you do is on a level with perfect, and I know it's from hard work and lots of years. But when you start talking about relationships, us specifically, I sense an insecurity which doesn't fit with the rest of your demeanor. I suspect it has something to do with your ex-wife. Tell me what happened?"

Nick was amazed at how perceptive she was. It was almost like she could read his soul. "I don't know there is much to tell. She burned me badly and I have been cautious ever since."

"When you hired me, I did some research about you," she said, blushing as he raised an eyebrow at her. "I wanted to know as much as I could since we were going to be spending a great deal of time together. I know it's been over twenty years since then. Maybe *cautious* isn't the right word. *Misogynistic* may be closer."

"That's harsh, love. I never stopped liking women, I just wasn't interested in getting burned again," he defended himself. "I've had a couple of other relationships since then, but being gone ten out of twelve months a year was hard on them. I'm here more, since I bought into the studio, but there was always the fame thing – everyone wants to say they were sleeping with me."

"So tell me anyway?" she asked quietly. She knew he needed to tell her this, even if he was denying it. "I'm sure it's a story I will hear at some point."

Nick made a silent decision, slipping out from under Kate, swinging his legs over the side of the bed. He turned on the lamp and pulled a cigarette from the pack next to it. Lighting it, he took a large drag and blew the smoke out slowly. "We were childhood friends, Sharon and I. She lived two doors down from me growing up. Her brother, Aaron, and I were best friends, so I was always over at their house since I didn't like being at mine."

"She was younger than you both?"

Nick smiled. "No, she was Aaron's twin. They were always together and eventually we three were always together. We officially started dating after I left school and moved out of my parent's house at sixteen to pursue my music. She was my fan club, always there to say things to make me feel better about myself and encouraged my music. We got married when we were twenty, mere days after I signed my first record contract - it was a real rough time. We probably should have waited to get married, but I was on cloud nine and thought we were on easy street.

"I was gone a lot of the time, recording, and then going with the studio folks to various television appearances, radio interviews, as well as my first tour in Britain. I was home maybe two weeks in a nine-month span. But at Christmas, I got to be home with her for two straight weeks and I think all we did was stay in bed. After the first of the year, I was off on a new tour, starting to hit some of the other European countries, France, Germany, Italy, and I got a call from her one night, excited to tell me she was pregnant with our child. It was a huge shock because I hadn't been thinking about having kids, at least not yet - I was totally wrapped up in my music. But we both knew I wouldn't let her abort it, so, in late August, Arianna Marie was born. And she was the image of her mother – brown hair, brown eyes."

Nick paused. He took the last drag off of the cigarette before stubbing it into the ashtray. "One of the rare times I was able to spend at home, we were watching television. Arianna, who was almost two, came running into the room, tripped, and fell into the glass coffee table, shattering it. She got a cut on her arm which wouldn't stop bleeding – it was really deep, so we rushed her to the hospital to have it stitched up. In the process, because she had lost a lot of blood, the doctors were talking about possibly doing a blood transfusion. They had her blood typed just in case. Out of curiosity, I asked one of the nurses what it was. I'm A-positive and Sharon was O-positive. The nurse looked at the chart and told me O-negative."

"Arianna wasn't your daughter," Kate whispered. She watched him light another cigarette.

"I didn't say anything to Sharon at first; I was trying to digest what I had heard. Because if she wasn't my daughter, then whose daughter was she? I stayed calm until we got Arianna back home and in bed before I confronted Sharon. After about an hour of lies, denials, and excuses, she finally owned up she had been sleeping with someone while I was gone. She tried to blame it on me for not being around but I was too angry to hear it. I didn't contain my temper then as well as I do now – I yelled and ranted at her for a good hour. I packed a bag, left in the middle of the night, and filed the divorce papers the next day. I gave her the house and her lawyers managed to get a stake of the money I had made while we were first married, but it was a one-time settlement and she had no claim over anything I did after. And, because she didn't want people to know we divorced due to her being unfaithful, Sharon didn't say anything to the press when they came knocking. She just cited irreconcilable differences, same as what I had been saying. She married Arianna's father shortly after the divorce was final and had a couple more kids, the last I knew."

"I'm sorry, Nick," she said softly, drawing light circles on his back with her fingers. "I didn't mean to hurt you."

"It doesn't hurt as much as it used to," he said. Putting out the cigarette, he slid back into bed and pulled Kate back to his chest. "With the other failed relationships, knowing they were all after my name and not me, I decided when the right woman came around, I would know. And you came walking into the studio set with Mickey and I knew. I wasn't going to act on it, but I knew."

"You never let on," Kate answered. "You were as cool as they come."

"I was frustrated out of my bloody mind is what I was. I was on day three of the auditions and there was nothing out there. I'd honestly thought I would have found my replacement the first afternoon."

"I walked out of the waiting room three times," she admitted to him. "I have never been scared to play in front of anyone, but my nerves kept telling me to leave."

"I probably wouldn't have auditioned you on the first day," he said honestly. "I didn't like to screen women for the simple reason I don't like the press which seems to go with it. I try very hard to keep a low profile so the tabloids have nothing to report about. "

"I can see why," she said, teasing him. "Look where it got you."

He smiled, lifting her chin to kiss her. "No complaints here, love. It's just been strange for me to be feeling this way."

"Me too," she said. "I am probably as relationship-phobic as you. At least you were getting something out of your failures – I didn't get past the first date on most of them."

"As pretty as you are, love? I find that hard to fathom."

"Never said they didn't try to share my bed, Nick. I wanted more than simple sex. I wanted something comfortable and close – not simply a wild time on a Saturday night."

"How do you know this isn't one of those?" he asked, his eyes dancing.

"You've had plenty of opportunities in the past six months if sex was all you wanted," Kate answered. "You didn't have to propose. And we don't have to get married, Nick – I won't force you into it."

"I've never felt this way about anyone. Including my ex-wife," he told her seriously. "The thought of not having you close invokes a terror I've never felt before."

Nick pulled her into his arms, holding her against him. With little effort, he swapped places with her, looking into her eyes as his mouth came down to meet hers. She returned his kiss and there was no more talking. The language of love was what they spoke for the rest of the evening, before falling asleep in each other's arms.

CHAPTER SEVEN

Kate drove into the city with Nick in the morning when he left for the studio. Her car was there from Monday; she wanted to get it and go out to her house. She followed him into the building and they rode up together in the elevator to his office, as he'd put her purse in his desk drawer for safe keeping. Nick's office was on the fifteenth floor, at the top of the building. It was supposed to be Jerry Santini's office – Jerry was Nick's partner with the studio – but Jerry said the view from the floor to ceiling windows gave him vertigo. Nick's office and a couple other meeting rooms were the only spaces on the floor. Terry, Nick's secretary, said she liked the view and had no problem working there. Nick introduced Kate then ushered her into his office, closing the door.

Nick pulled Kate's purse out of his desk drawer and handed it over to her. "Sorry, I didn't think to bring it to you, love. I was a little shortsighted on Monday."

"It's all good," she told him. "Wasn't like I needed it."

"What are you going to do today?" he asked.

"Run a few loads of laundry, maybe go by my mom's house and check in, since I've been gone for six months."

Nick paused for a moment. "Come back to the house later?" he asked, hesitantly. "We can have the weekend together."

Kate nodded. "It would be nice."

Nick wrote a number on a piece of note paper and handed it to Kate. "Here's the code for the front gate."

Kate folded it up and put it in her pocket. "Call me when you leave?"

Nick came around his desk to stand in front of Kate. He pulled her close to him and kissed her. "I'll call," he promised. "It's going to be a long day."

* * *

Kate left the studio and drove home. Once home, she retrieved both of her suitcases from her bedroom and took them into the laundry room. It took her fifteen minutes to sort everything into the proper loads and she started the first one in the washer. There was a nice breeze blowing outside and Kate opened the windows in her living room, letting the sea air permeate the stuffy room. She heard her cell phone buzz and saw she had a text message from Nick.

It's official – it's going to be a really long day.

That bad? Kate asked.

The soundboard in studio three caught fire –that was entertaining. And if the fire wasn't enough, the drummer and bass player for the group Mark Three got into a fist fight over a woman this morning. Bass player got his nose broken.

Kate started to laugh; she could picture the look on Nick's face right now. *Sounds like you are having a fun, eventful day.*

Any more fun and I'll be in a nut house.

Once the laundry was finished, Kate called her mom to confirm she would be home, before driving out to Westwood where they lived. Kate pulled her car into the driveway behind her step-dad's, glad he was home too. Allen had been more of a father to her than her own dad and she enjoyed spending time with him. She got a big hug from him when she came in the door and her mom whisked her away into the kitchen. Kate sat down at the breakfast bar, watching her mom pour two cups of coffee, and setting one in front of her.

"We missed you, baby," Nancy, Kate's mom, started. "Six months was a long time to be gone."

Kate nodded. "It was a long time. But it was good – hard work, though."

"So you're going to continue working for Nick Marshall?"

"For now," Kate confirmed. "It was a challenging experience. Nick's a perfectionist and it shows when he's on tour."

"You didn't have any problems did you?" Nancy asked.

"Nothing major. It took me about a month to get used to the pace. Sometimes I would hit the bed so tired at night."

"But you like the job, right?"

"I do," Kate answered, and paused for a moment to gather her thoughts. "Nick and I are starting to see each other."

"You mean like boy-girl kind of seeing?"

Kate laughed at her mom's description. "Yes, Mom, boy-girl kind of seeing. We didn't start off this way – we've just found we're attracted to each other."

"Isn't he a lot older than you?" Nancy asked.

"Not so much. Thirteen years – Nick's forty-six."

"He's your boss."

"I know," Kate confirmed. "Nick's having the same issue. He sees it not much different than a manager dating his secretary – we are working through the pieces slowly."

Allen stepped up behind Kate. "I asked Michael Grayson about him when you first took the job. See what kind of man he was, reputation. He has a powerful name and tons of money."

"They work at competing studios," Kate said. "Did he have anything nice to say about Nick?"

"A lot actually," Allen replied, surprising her. "He said it's been Nick turning Empire Records around. They were starting to see a lot of losses and it was looking bad for a while. And his own popularity hasn't diminished. Michael said you don't see that often in singers who have been in the business a long time."

"Most places were completely sold out. Nick even added a bunch of extra shows to try to meet the demand. And, the crazy thing is, most of the fans there are girls between seventeen and twenty-five, screaming his name like he's some young teen idol," Kate told them.

"Michael also said he didn't know how Nick was able to juggle both. The studio business is demanding on its own."

"He spent a good portion of his time on the phone with them when we were touring, so I think he's pretty engaged. He was funny on the phone this morning – seems it's been one of the 'everything goes wrong' kind of days."

As if on cue, Kate's cell phone started to ring. She saw it was from Nick and excused herself, walking away into the living room to answer it.

"Hello."

"It's me, love. I am heading home now – almost to my car."

"I'm at my mom's house. She lives in Westwood, so I'll be a few extra minutes," Kate told him.

"No problem. I'll leave the front door unlocked – got a key made for you this morning."

"Want me to bring anything? Pizza, Chinese?"

"I never turn away good Chinese takeout," Nick said. "Just don't get anything too spicy."

"I'll be there soon."

Kate walked back into the kitchen. "That was Nick. Need to go get some food and then meet him."

"Come for dinner on Sunday?" Nancy asked. "You can bring Nick if you want."

"Let me ask him and I'll let you know," Kate said, moving to kiss her mom on the cheek then giving her step-dad a hug. "If not, I'll be here for another two weeks. I'll make sure to come by again before I leave."

Kate left and stopped by her favorite Chinese food place in Long Beach. She had been going there for the past six years, ever since she started working at Satellite Records. Some of the studio guys recommended it and now it was the only place she liked to get takeout from. She opted for fried rice, beef and broccoli, and chicken chow mein. She also ordered some wontons and a couple of egg rolls. The biggest reason she liked this place was they packaged their food in the little boxes, rather than the styrofoam containers many restaurants like to use. Despite her age, Kate always found it more fun to eat it from the little boxes.

At Nick's house, she punched in the four-digit code he had given her and the gate opened, allowing her to drive up the driveway. She parked next to Nick's car in the large garage - he had left a space for her. She walked in through the front door, heading to the kitchen to put the food down.

"Nick," she called.

"Be right there, love," he answered from upstairs.

Kate started unpacking the food. She had the restaurant put everything in larger boxes, so you could add the rice and the other entrée and still eat out of the container. Searching the drawers, she found both the silverware and the serving spoons. Using one of the large spoons, she split both entrées into the rice boxes and pulled out a fork in case Nick wanted one - she had no issue eating the whole meal with the chopsticks, it was part of the fun. Looking in the refrigerator, she saw Consuelo had made ice tea and she pulled the pitcher out, putting it on the counter. Another search and she found where the glasses were kept, next to the sink, and she pulled two out. The ice dispenser was in the refrigerator door, and she made it a quick task, putting ice in both glasses then filling them with tea. Six months of eating dinner at the same table had told Kate he liked his ice tea without sugar, same as she did.

Nick came around the corner and smiled at the meal she had put together. He draped his arm over her shoulder to distract her as he tried to snatch one of the wontons. Kate laughed at the innocent expression he tried to adopt when he got caught red handed. "This is awesome," he confirmed, finishing it in two bites. "And I'm starving."

"Fork or chopsticks?" Kate asked.

"Chopsticks, of course," he answered, and she handed him a box and a pair of chopsticks.

Kate also handed him a glass of tea, picked up her own food and drink, and followed Nick outside to the covered porch he had coming off the kitchen. Nick had a large swimming pool and there was a rock path leading down to the ocean. The porch was covered to help keep out the hot California sun.

"This is beautiful, Nick."

"I bought it for the serenity," he told her. "I needed somewhere I could go which was both pleasing to look at and secluded."

"You definitely got it. Sounded like you needed it earlier."

"Love, you have no idea," he answered, rolling his eyes. "It didn't help I flat out didn't want to be there. How was the visit to your parents?"

"It was good," she said, smiling. "They invited us to dinner on Sunday."

"You told them about us?"

"I told them the truth. We are starting into a relationship – I can't hide personal stuff from them. And I don't know I would want to."

"I'm not sure I'm ready for the parent thing yet, Kate," he told her, his tone a little hesitant.

"It's fine. I told them I would ask you – I didn't commit you to anything."

Nick was silent for a few minutes, eating the food expertly with the chopsticks. "It's something you would like to do, though, isn't it?"

Kate looked at him intently. "Nick, if you are uncomfortable about this because the whole family thing is new to you, I can be good with it. But if you are out of sorts because I told them about us, then we dealing with a totally different issue. And one I'm not sure won't be detrimental to us."

Kate got up and went inside, throwing her almost empty carton into the trash can. Her first thought was to just keep walking out the door and leave. Kate was very close to her parents and something as important as their relationship was something she wanted them to know. She had kept it very low key – she shouldn't have had to tell him as much – and his comment about being a difficult bastard came back to her. Right now she could see the truth in it as clearly as a bright blue sky. Kate knew they would probably have a lot of these kinds of conversations until they reached some kind of a comfortable relationship - which is why she didn't walk.

Kate cleaned up the mess she had made and was hanging the dish towel over the handle on the oven door, where Consuelo normally kept it, when Nick walked back in. He threw his empty container in the trash and leaned in the doorway, looking at Kate. She stood with her back to the sink, finishing the iced tea and waiting for him to start the conversation. She appreciated he didn't come in and immediately try to hug her to make it go away.

"Would it help if I told you the thought of meeting your parents makes me nervous?" he started.

"I can understand those feelings. And the truth is they invited me and said you were welcome to come if you wanted. Make you feel better?"

"Some. Doesn't make me feel like they want to size me up, make sure I fit their expectations."

Kate wasn't about to tell him about what Michael Grayson had told her dad. "I don't think you'll have any issues, Nick. My step-dad works in a corporate environment – he deals with important people all the time."

"The last time I sat down at the dinner table with family was when I was sixteen," he told her. "And it turned into a yelling match with my dad. I packed up and left the same night."

"Sixteen was pretty young to be out on your own," she observed.

"Worked a lot of odd jobs until I got one as a busboy in a nightclub in London. As soon as I convinced my boss to let me audition to play in the club, my busboy days were gone. That's how I started, love. And it has been my own hard work to be where I am now."

Kate set her glass in the sink and walked over to Nick, putting her arms around him. "It's fine if you don't want to go. Someday you won't feel that way."

"No," he said in a definite tone. "We'll go. Not all the compromises in this relationship are yours. I'll have plenty of my own."

"You're sure?"

Nick nodded, pulling her tight against him. "I'm sure, love," he answered, his mouth finding hers. His kiss was insistent, telling her he needed this confirmation –his meeting her on this had pleased her in the only way she could tell him. Words were not always enough – sometimes actions were needed for confirmation.

* * *

Nick and Kate arrived at her parent's house on Sunday around three o'clock. Kate had him pull his car into the driveway and the garage door was open. In the garage was a baby-blue, 1957 Thunderbird which was in a state of remodel. This was her step-dad's pet project – he had been restoring it for the past two years. There was music playing and, since she couldn't see him, Kate was certain he was under the car working on something. Nick walked over, lightly running his hand on the body of the car, almost in a state of awe.

"Dad?"

"Under here, Kate," Allen answered.

After a minute, her step-dad came rolling out from under the car. He stood up, wiping his hands on a shop towel to make sure there was no oil on them before putting one out to Nick. "Allen Thomas," he said.

"Nick Marshall," Nick answered, and the two men shook hands. "This is a beautiful machine you have here."

"You like cars?" he asked.

"Love old ones; just don't have the time to do anything like this. The car would be on blocks for years."

"Grab the other creeper against the wall and I'll show you what I was doing."

Nick brought the other creeper over and slid under the car with Allen. Kate shook her head, laughing as she walked into the house.

* * *

Allen spent the better part of an hour with Nick, first underneath the car showing him the restorations he had done and the rest from the top. Nick loved old cars but he knew his schedule would never allow him a project such as this. And he got so involved in the time with Allen, he forgot he had ever been nervous about coming over in the first place.

"Okay," Allen started, smiling. "I am going to put my 'Dad' hat on now and ask the main 'Dad' question. What are your intentions with my daughter?"

"I love your daughter," Nick said, without hesitating, smiling at the question. "No ifs, ands, buts, or maybes about it."

"There are a lot of hurdles you both are going to have to cross. The biggest one, I think, is she works for you."

"It is the big one," Nick agreed. "We didn't start out this way. Matter of fact, I made sure we didn't have a lot of face time, so there would be no blurring of the lines. That theory shattered to pieces, however."

"You know what happened to her with her ex-husband?" Allen asked.

"I know," Nick said. "She ran into him in New York and there was an altercation in the hotel lobby. I made a call to London and got him pulled out of New York, but the damage was already done."

"I'm just giving you a hard time about the 'dad' thing – Kate is an adult and can make her own decisions. And I'm only her step-dad, so it doesn't have much weight."

"I think you carry more than you think," Nick told him. "And I can understand your concerns, but Kate is the first woman I have even thought about seriously in over twenty years. I'm sure the tabloids have said differently."

"I don't read tabloids," he answered. "My clients run into a lot of trouble with them at times and then I have to defend against them, which I despise. I didn't get into corporate law to argue the first amendment at every turn."

"That's okay, mate. I didn't get into music to spend my life on their front page either."

Allen started to laugh. "Let go inside. I'm sure my wife is anxious to meet you and dinner should about be ready."

* * *

Kate had left the two men talking underneath the thunderbird, going into the house. "Hi, Mom," she said, as she saw her setting the table for dinner.

"Hey, baby," she answered. Nancy paused, looking around. "Thought you were bringing Nick."

"I did," Kate laughed. "He's under the T-bird with Dad."

Nancy laughed with her. "Well, there's a good sign."

"Didn't know he was into old cars," Kate said. "But then there's a lot I don't know about him."

"It's all part of the process, getting to know them," she said. "It took Allen three tries before I would even go to dinner with him."

"You didn't like him?

"I liked him fine. I thought lawyers were stuffy and I didn't want a boring dinner date."

"Well, personally I'm glad you went on that date," Kate confirmed. "He's fantastic."

"So give me some background – any subjects I need stay away from?"

"I wouldn't ask him family related questions unless he opens the conversation," Kate said. "He's been on his own since he was a teenager because he was estranged from them. His dad recently died and it was a nightmare for him to go home and bury him."

"On the subject of family, have you told him?" Nancy asked.

"Not yet," Kate said. "Relationship is still too new. And I'm not sure he even wants any kids, as busy as he is."

"You need to be straight with him, Kate," her mom said, in a definite tone. "Before this gets too much further along. I don't want to see you invest a lot into this and have it go sour because you didn't tell him. And it will cause issues with any professional relationship with him as well."

"I'll tell him," she confirmed. "Right now getting married is his answer to working through the boss/employee block he has. Not sure it's what either of us wants to do yet."

"Would you have time to do that before you leave again?" Nancy asked.

"With two weeks left, possibly. I personally would rather wait until we got back, but it will put a strain on things because he won't share a suite with me on the road. That's the nature of the hang up with him. And he won't budge."

"You've slept together then?" Nancy asked.

Kate blushed. "Didn't plan it, but yes. And we've been together every night since."

"This is 2014, Kate, not the 1960's. Sex before marriage is no longer frowned upon."

"I can't believe we're having this conversation," Kate said, laughing, half to herself.

"What conversation?" Allen asked, as he and Nick came into the kitchen.

"Never mind, Dad," Kate answered. "Mom, this is Nick. Nick, this is my mom, Nancy."

Her mom went over and put her hand out for a handshake. "I'm glad to meet you," she said warmly.

Nick towered over her – Nancy was only five-foot-three. He took her hand in his and kissed it. "I'm glad to meet you, too."

"I am surprised you two came out from under the car without prodding," Kate said.

"Even mechanics get hungry," her dad answered. "Nick's going to come help me pull the engine next weekend."

Kate rolled her eyes. "Well, that's it then. I guess I've lost you to my dad."

Nick smiled. "Only temporarily, love."

Nancy began putting the food on the table and Kate went in to help. Allen and Nick sat down at the table, waiting for everything to be brought out. Kate placed a glass of tea in front of Nick and, looking at him, he seemed calm – she hadn't expected him to be so. Once everything was in place, the women sat down, each across from their man.

Conversation started lightly, but it didn't take long for Nick to get engaged. Kate had been right – Nick did have a lot in common with her step-father and their discussions about corporate topics more than confirmed it. Kate was glad he was getting comfortable enough to respond – Nick could be frustratingly quiet when he wasn't. And he had been tense about coming, just based on the fact the idea of family was foreign to him. Kate could see her parents genuinely liked him for him and his being a famous musician never played into the conversation. They treated him no differently than they would have any other date Kate may have brought to dinner. In Kate's opinion, Nick needed that kind of open acceptance.

JEANINE BINDER

CHAPTER EIGHT

Nick brought up getting married again just before the next weekend. There was no wait time to get married in California – the state only required a marriage license which could take up to two hours to get. Nick wasn't interested in sitting at city hall for two hours – he wanted to take a quick hop to Las Vegas, where they could do so much more efficiently.

Kate was quiet as she lay against his chest. She remembered what her mom said and knew she had come to a crossroad. "I need to tell you something, Nick."

"That sounds ominous," Nick said, sliding out from under her. He sat on the side of the bed and lit a cigarette. "What's wrong?"

"How important is it for you to have children?" Kate asked.

"It's never been on the top of the list of things I want in my life," Nick told her. "I know it sounds fairly callous, but I don't know if I'd want to start a family at this age in my life. I'd be almost seventy before they graduated high school."

"It needs to be something you are certain on, one direction or the other," she said, her voice dropping almost to a whisper. "Because if we continue with this relationship, you won't have any."

"Then we don't have any," Nick answered, his tone certain. "I love you, Kate, and if we can't have any, then so be it."

"You're sure?"

"As sure as I can be, love," Nick replied. He took a large drag off of the cigarette, blowing it out slowly. "It doesn't matter, but why?"

"Remember the fall I told you about, when my ex pushed me down the stairs?" Kate asked, watching his eyes change, seeing the anger starting to well up. She hadn't known he was still emotional about this. "The part I withheld was I was pregnant when it happened. I lost the baby and the fallout caused the doctors to do a full hysterectomy to stop the internal bleeding."

"Did he know you were pregnant when he pushed you?" Nick asked, his voice almost staccato as he asked the question.

Kate shook her head. "I hadn't worked up the courage to tell him. We argued all the time by then and I was afraid of his reaction."

"Makes me wish I'd had the conversation in New York. The one where he ended up on the floor in a few pieces," Nick answered.

Kate got up and moved behind Nick, hugging him. "Don't let it get you all worked up, Nick. It was a long time ago."

"Kate, it's just brutal what he did. It wasn't bad enough he destroyed everything you had dreamed of since you were a kid. He caused your child to die – killed the life growing in you and got away with murder."

"My parents wanted to press charges for the baby," Kate said softly. "I told them to let it go. I wanted out of the marriage and him out of my life. If I took him to court, it would've been months of added anguish I didn't want."

Nick's cell phone started ringing. Nick looked at it and swore as he picked it up off the nightstand. "Marshall," he said answering it. He stood up and walked out of the room.

Kate was feeling better now he knew she couldn't have children. It had been weighing heavily on her mind since he had shared the story of Arianna with her. For her, she had made peace with it – it was part of the reason most of her previous dates had remained as first or second dates. The guys she dated were her age, looking to start married life and have a family. She had been fairly certain Nick would respond this way, but there was always a chance he wouldn't have been happy. Relief flooded through her. Now she was worried about who was on the phone. Nick obviously knew who it was when he saw the number, but it didn't sound promising.

* * *

Nick came back in and tossed the phone on the bed. Reaching for his clothes on the chair, he began to get dressed. "I have to go, love," Nick started, pulling on the pants he wore earlier.

"What's the matter?"

"Jaime Garwood got arrested for assault. I have to go down with Greg Sullen, the studio attorney, and fix this mess."

Jamie Garwood was a new addition to the studio. Like Nick was twenty-five years ago, Jamie was turning out to be the next music heartthrob. The only problem was he was all ego and thought he was quite the lady killer. He also had a problem with women telling him no when it came to sex; in his immature mind, because of who he was becoming, they should be glad to sleep with him. Unfortunately, when they told him no, his impulsive nature was to use force and almost rape them. This wasn't the first time he had been in jail – nor was it the first time Nick had to try to keep it hushed up in the press.

"Do you want me to come with you?"

"I'd love it, except that I don't want you down at the police station and associated with this," Nick said grimly. "The kid is outstandingly talented. He just doesn't have the maturity needed to be as famous as he is."

"I'll keep your place warm," Kate said invitingly.

"I'll be back to claim it," he agreed, pausing to kiss her. Then he strode out of the room and Kate heard the front door close, followed by the sound of his car starting up.

* * *

As it worked out, Kate and Nick didn't get a chance to set up any kind of wedding during the break. It took all of Nick's skill and resources to keep Jamie's arrest out of the newspapers. He and Greg had been able to get him off on a plea deal, which consisted of anger management classes and a lot of community service, including a concert which would benefit a battered women's shelter. The studio had lawyers on staff for this kind of thing as musicians tended to act like little kids sometimes and the studio didn't want to take the hit. It frustrated Nick all of his time was going to fix this and before he knew it, there were two days before the European tour. And there would be no time for him and Kate to do anything.

Kate and Nick discussed it over dinner at her townhouse on Saturday night. Both agreed for now, they would continue as before. "It's fine, Nick," Kate told him. "Another three months doesn't matter. It won't change how I feel about you."

"I know," Nick answered. "I was hoping to not have to use separate rooms."

Kate blushed a little. "We don't have to, you know. We can tell the band the truth and they won't think badly of either of us."

"It's not them, love. It's me," Nick admitted. "I am still having issues over the whole boss versus employee notion. Until I put the ring on your finger, I'm not going to have you dragged through the press as my willing mistress."

"I can't be your mistress, Nick. You'd have to have a wife for me to be your mistress," she said, teasing him.

Nick shot her a look. "You know what I mean. And I just wanted to smack Garwood during this whole thing. His arrogance irritates the bloody hell out of me."

"He should be appreciative," Kate said. "Personally, I think some time in a jail cell might have cooled him off."

"Here's where being a businessman sucks. His being in jail had an opportunity cost I didn't want to explore."

"I'm sure it added to the arrogance. He knew you weren't going to go against him."

"I made it more than abundantly clear I would if it happens again," Nick said, in a hard tone. "Next time he pulls this crap, I'm pulling the contract. I don't want the negative press and I don't need the headache."

"Jerry's going to let you do that? Jamie's pretty hot right now."

"Jerry has no say in this. We set up the partnership so we are responsible for our own agreements. I signed Garwood so he's my problem. And Jamie doesn't want to push that far – I have the pull to make sure he never records again in this industry and I made it *crystal* clear."

Kate got up from the table, taking the dishes and things back to the kitchen. "Are you planning to stay here tonight?" she asked, changing the subject.

"If you want me to," Nick said, as he followed her. He stood watching her from the doorway, not sure what prompted the question. They had been inseparable at night since they got back. "You could always pack up and come home with me."

"I do need to pack," Kate agreed. "I was going to finish some laundry and do it tomorrow."

"I'll stay and help you get yours done. Then you can come help me with mine. Nothing I hate more than packing a suitcase."

"As much as you're gone?" Kate said in disbelief. "I'd have thought you were an old hand at it by now."

"Didn't say I couldn't do it efficiently," Nick said, watching her load the dishwasher. "Just said I hated doing it."

The buzzer for the dryer went off. "Well, there's part of it done," she said, closing the door to the dishwasher and walking away to the laundry room which was behind the kitchen. She folded the clothes on the table in the room and put the load from the washer into the dryer. Kate figured she'd leave the clean clothes on the table and pack one suitcase from there, rather than take it all upstairs.

* * *

She came back in from the laundry room, looking for Nick and found him on the couch with the television remote, flipping through channels. He patted a spot in front of him on the couch and Kate went to him, sitting down cross-legged and snuggling back against his chest. "Doesn't appear to be anything worth watching," Nick commented.

"I know," she agreed. "I usually only watch the Food Network or the Dodgers if they're playing."

"I saw a game," he said, flipping back to a Dodgers baseball game.

"Didn't know you liked baseball."

"I'm not much into sports period," he admitted. "I would rather just talk to you."

"Sounds good," Kate said. "Television has become background noise at best these days."

There was silence for a few minutes. Kate quickly saw the Dodgers were ahead, which pleased her since she was a big fan. She could sense Nick was putting some big thoughts together so she remained quiet, more than happy to spend the time with him. There was so much they didn't know about each other – a lifetime's worth for both.

"This is so odd for me," Nick said finally.

"What is?"

"My last serious relationship with anyone was over eight years ago," he began. "I met an actress at a studio party."

"Melanie Albertson," Kate prompted. "It's not a big secret, Nick."

"She was pretty, had a good sense of humor, and she understood the stress of having a famous name. We were both busy people so our time together had to be planned. I used to think it was part of the problem; if I had to plan to spend the night with her, all sense of spontaneity was gone. I simply didn't feel anything for her, short of being her friend."

Nick stopped for a moment and Kate continued to lean back against his chest, aware of the arm holding her there. Nick wasn't usually forthcoming about information unless he was specifically asked so she patiently waited for him to continue. "She ended it after about six months. Said she never saw us as anything more than friends and she needed more. I didn't disagree; I knew she was right. But then you come along with a late night story of heartache, pain, and terror and all I wanted to do was wrap my arms around you and try to take some of it. And I really wanted to go drag your ex out of his hotel suite and beat the bloody hell out of him for what he did, and I'm not normally a physical kind of person."

"It's ancient history, Nick," Kate said softly. "I've had ten years to get past it and I think I have."

"I know. But the crazy thing is I think about you all the time. I never did with Melanie, or anyone else for that matter. Including Sharon and I thought it was love at its fullest. I want to protect you, take care of you, be there for you. I have never felt this way about a single person in my life."

"Maybe for the first time, you are truly in love," Kate said thoughtfully. "I know I feel so much more for you than I ever did when I was dating Kevin or when we were married. I wanted to come through the phone when you were in London and try to stop the pain. I wasn't sure how you felt about me, but I didn't care."

"I wasn't sure then either," Nick admitted. "I knew I liked you and I knew you were someone I could get close to, but I wasn't sure I wanted to take that step. I'd been pretty definite about not getting married again. I'd been pretty definite about not wanting to let a woman in my life again, period. That theory flew out the window when you walked into the room, wrapping your arms around me. It stopped me cold and I wanted you to stay very badly."

"I'd listened to you for three nights straight, trying to sound like you were in control, and it was obvious you weren't. Having lost my own father, I had firsthand experience of what grief felt like. But, based on what I knew about your family, I could feel your pain, Nick, like it was my own."

Nick wrapped his arms around her tighter. "This is going to be a hard three months, love. And I will tell you I'm sorry now, but I can't to do this any other way. We shouldn't have spent these past three weeks together either, but I'm not quite that noble."

"It will add to the strength of our relationship," Kate said. "If we can't weather this, then we don't have any business going any further." She paused for a moment. "But I will be slightly disappointed if there isn't a plane to Vegas or something equivalent within a few days of getting back."

"I think I can get it arranged. What about your family? Aren't they going to want to be there?"

"They didn't come when I married Kevin and it was a civil ceremony. They will probably want to celebrate with us in some way though."

The dryer buzzed in the other room and Nick released his hold so Kate could go take care of it. She folded the rest of the clothes and came back into the living room. She walked over to Nick and held her hand out to him. He turned off the television and got up, letting Kate lead him to the stairs and up to the second floor. Once in Kate's bedroom, Nick stopped and pulled her to him, his mouth finding hers in a demanding kiss. Kate knew his sharing had affected him, making him less gentle, but she returned the kiss without hesitation. He picked her up, putting her on the bed and started the act of undressing her. His mouth never left hers, insistent and probing, and soon both were oblivious to the real world, enveloped in their need for each other.

* * *

Kate was dead tired as she walked with the rest of the band into the hotel and to the elevator. Between the time change from Los Angeles to London, and then having to be at the Hall by eight, Kate's mental time schedule was all messed up and she had a bad case of jet lag. All she wanted to do was crash – she wasn't hungry or interested in going anywhere with the rest of the guys. She bid them all good night, scanned the key card Mickey had given her and went into her room. It was a normal one bedroom suite – the kind of room she was used to at this point. She turned the light on in the sitting room for Brock, set her backpack over by the closet and started to walk into the bedroom. Out of nowhere a hand grabbed her and pulled her against a hard chest. She could feel the metal of the knife at her throat.

"Don't move," the voice said, and Kate knew it was Kevin behind her.

"What do you want from me, Kevin?"

"I want you and I have wasted the better part of ten years looking for you. No one walks away from me."

"You pushed me down a flight of stairs and smashed my hand," Kate said, fear and anger making her bold enough to argue with him. "You ruined my dream and my career. Why would I want to stay with you?"

"You vowed," he reminded her. "Until death. So this is the plan: we are going to walk out of here nice and quietly."

"Kevin, there's no way Nick's security is going to let us out of the hotel. You're crazy to even think it," Kate said.

"They either let us go or I'll slit your throat," Kevin said against her ear. "Let's go."

The sound of a key card in the door froze Kevin in place. Kevin pulled Kate tighter against him and held the knife closer, watching as the door opened and Brock walked in. Kevin moved Kate a few steps into the room and Brock stopped still. Kate could feel the knife starting to draw blood against her neck.

"So this is your lover?" he sneered, not realizing Brock was security. "Going for seconds, I see. I'd have thought you wouldn't have settled for less than Marshall himself. Wish I had known in New York. We could have fixed this then."

"Kate, don't move," Brock said, taking a step closer.

"Don't do it big boy," Kevin said. "I will kill her before you can yell."

Kate looked at Brock; they had prepared for a situation exactly like this. He nodded at her ever so slightly and Kate went limp in Kevin's grasp. Kevin was set off balance for a second and it was enough for Brock to come barreling at him, knocking him to the floor. They kept Kate cut off from the door and her heart was in her throat as she watched the two men wrestle for control. She started to yell – hoping someone would hear her - and suddenly Kevin gave a shout of exultation as she saw him stab Brock in his left leg. Something came over her, as Kevin started to pull himself back up and Kate shoved him, hard, up against the wall, causing his head to slam into it. He slumped to the floor.

Between Kate's yelling and the slamming of Kevin into the wall, Sam and Kyle came running in. Security always had a master key card for all the rooms. Kate was on the floor with Brock, hands on his thigh trying to stop the bleeding. It was pouring out of his leg and it was obvious the knife had slashed something important. Kate slipped her fingers into the wound – Brock was doing everything he could to hold still, obviously knowing she was trying to help as he went in and out of consciousness. She found the artery which was bleeding and pinched it with her fingers, the bleeding barely slowing to a trickle. Sam was standing over Kevin and Kyle was on the phone to get both an ambulance and the police.

"Stay still, Brock," Kate said to him softly. "I have the artery between my fingers and I'm not letting go. Ambulance is coming."

"Bloody hell," another voice said from the doorway and Kate glanced up long enough to see Nick enter the room. She didn't pay him much attention – all of her composure was focused on keeping Brock alive, but she did get a look at his face as he walked around the unconscious Kevin. Kate had blood all over her neck, shirt, and pants and she watched Nick look her over. She was sure it was impossible to know how much of it was hers and how much was Brock's.

"Kate," was all he said. Kate could easily see Nick was upset - he didn't say much but she could see the dark look on his face. His rage was contained but Kate knew he was walking a tight edge. Nick didn't deal well when things quit going as planned and the fact she was involved, Kate knew, was making this even more difficult for him.

"He was waiting in the room and jumped me," was all Kate said. The paramedics walked in and Kate still held the artery clamped. The paramedics didn't have anything in their kit they were confident would do a better job and asked her if she would come with them. Kate nodded and they loaded Brock onto a gurney and they left for the hospital. The police had been right behind them and they handcuffed Kevin just as he was coming around. The police took a statement from Sam and Kyle, but both told them they needed to get the actual events from Kate and Brock.

CHAPTER NINE

Once at the hospital, doctors were able to clamp off Brock's artery so Kate could release it. Stepping back, she looked down and saw the enormous amount of blood on her shirt and her pants, now understanding the look Nick had given her back in the hotel room. *This has to be scaring the crap out of him; to have seen this and not been able to react.* Kate thought this might push him over the edge and break down his mental block. Thankfully Kevin hadn't been interested in actually doing bodily harm otherwise he could have killed her before Brock ever walked in the room. She still didn't understand what was mentally driving her ex-husband. His obsession didn't make sense because he tried to drive her away emotionally before the accident ever happened. Ten years later, he had the career he wanted and she should have been old news.

One of the nurses saw her expression and came over. She told Kate to follow her and walked them to where they kept clean scrubs for the hospital staff. Pulling out a set she took Kate down to shower and change. Kate knew there was no salvaging either the pants or the shirt, and trashed them in the proper container for blood-contaminated items. The nurse stayed until she was done and noticed the cut on her neck was still seeping. It wasn't deep enough for stitches but there was still some blood coming to the surface so the nurse put some antiseptic ointment on it and covered it with a clean bandage. Kate followed the nurse out to the waiting room, as the doctors had taken Brock up to surgery.

When Kate got into the waiting room, she saw all the band members, half the security force, and even Nick himself. Nick being there surprised her; she knew how much he tried to stay out of the public eye while on tour and she was touched that he would be there for Brock... and her. She took a moment to gauge his expression before making her presence known – she wasn't sure if it was worry or anger on his face; probably a mixture of both. Kate came walking up and smiled weakly at everyone. Trent was the first one to see her, jumping up to give her a brotherly bear hug, and the other three guys joined in. Nick stayed in the foreground and Kate knew it was because he didn't want to give anything away to the rest of the group.

"I'm okay guys, really," Kate said, as they let her go. "And it's sweet you came out here."

"Wouldn't have missed it," Trent said. "Ready to go back to the hotel?"

Kate shook her head. "You guys can head back. I'd like to stay until Brock is out of surgery."

"What happened in the room, love?" Nick asked, his voice deceptively soft as he walked over to her.

"Kevin was waiting for me in the bathroom. I had walked into the sitting room, turned the light on for Brock, and was heading to the bedroom. He grabbed me and put a knife to my throat."

It was nice to have so many guys as makeshift brothers because the air in the room got decidedly more heated. Kate glanced at Nick, never before seeing such a look of controlled anger on anyone's face before.

"Brock and I have been busy since New York," she added, with a smile. "He'd been teaching me self-defense moves after the altercation in New York. I was afraid Kevin would try again, especially now he knew how to find me. We had practiced for this kind of situation, ironic as that is. We had a signal which made me go limp. When I used it, I threw Kevin off balance and Brock lunged for him. Brock almost got the knife away before Kevin got the upper hand and stabbed him in the thigh with it. I lost it and threw myself at Kevin, slamming him into the wall. Sam and Kyle came in at that point and you guys know the rest. But I think he went at Brock harder because he thought I was sleeping with him."

"Why do you think that?" Sam asked.

"Kevin made a snide comment about Nick. He was totally convinced in New York the only reason Nick had hired me was because I was sleeping with him and he sounded surprised when he thought I had chosen Brock instead. It was those kinds of comments, among other things, which led to our divorce in the first place."

The surgeon who had been working on Brock entered the waiting room, looking for family. Kate jumped up and all but ran to him to hear the prognosis, which, thankfully, was good. Kate asked to see him and the doctor agreed reluctantly. Kate walked back over to the group to let them know what the doctor had said.

"Brock's going to be all right," she announced and cheers went up. "The doctor is going to let me go see him. You guys probably ought to head back to the hotel - I can follow later."

Kate watched Nick whisper something to Sam, who then walked over to Kate's side. She knew he had told Sam to remain. The rest of the group wanted to stay as well, but Kate convinced all but Andy to go back, agreeing to wait with Sam while she went in to see Brock. She really wanted Nick to stay but knew it was out of the question. She was comfortable with Andy; he had assumed the role of her mentor in the beginning, helping her adjust to the touring environment, advising her with the first shows. Nick smiled at her as he walked away with the others but Kate saw it didn't reach his eyes – she knew he was a ticking time bomb. There was no avoiding this blow out – she almost felt bad for security because they were who Nick was going to focus his anger on. Kate watched him walk out the door and then followed the surgeon, leaving Sam and Andy to wait for her.

"Hey," she said softly, once in the recovery room with Brock. He was awake but clearly still out of it. He looked like a machine from a science fiction movie, with tubes running in and out, including one as a drain in his leg.

"Hey," he answered hoarsely, taking in the bandage on her neck. "Are you all right?"

"I'm fine. You're the one with all the extra work," she teased, motioning to everything around him.

"Glad those self-defense lessons paid off," Brock said smiling. "Kate, please tell Sam not to call my wife. She'll just freak."

"I'll tell him," she said, bending over to kiss his cheek. "Doctor said I could only stay a minute, but I'll come back in the morning."

He nodded, closing his eyes to go to sleep. Kate left the recovery room and Andy draped his arm over her shoulders to walk her out. Andy was the oldest of Nick's band members and had been with Nick almost since the beginning. Kate regarded him like a big brother and was glad he was there - her nerves were a little frayed. She gave Sam the message from Brock; he didn't look like he agreed but said he would abide by it for now.

* * *

The next morning, Nick had most of his security people in the main room with him and told the rest of the band to go find other things to do. With his tone of voice, the band had left immediately and didn't look back. The fact Kate's ex was able to not only get on the floor but hide out in her room was unacceptable and Nick was more than angry. It showed on his face, in his tone, and there had been very little conversation at breakfast. No one wanted to set that explosion off.

All the security guys, except Ryan and Mike, and, of course, Brock, stood silently while Nick raged at them about the incident for the better part of an hour. Ryan was absent as he had accompanied Kate back to the hospital and Mike was watching the floor to keep unwanted people off this level. Nick was worried about Kate; she was being extremely calm about the whole thing and this kind of silence usually meant something else was building up on the inside. The separation they maintained put Nick at a severe disadvantage last night. All he had wanted was to go wrap his arms around her and keep her safe. Instead, he spent a very sleepless and anxious night, the two only serving to fuel his temper to a mountain high level this morning.

"So how did he get in?" Nick demanded, once he felt his point was made.

"Maids let him in," Sam said. "He tipped one really big and showed her a picture of him and Kate together ten years ago. She believed he was her husband, come to surprise her on her birthday."

"Sam, you need to talk to the hotel manager. We need to keep this as quiet as possible."

Sam nodded. "We talked last night; he has no interest in having a bunch of press in here asking questions. He's also going to address the issue with the maid."

"What have you heard from the police?"

"Scotland Yard still has Miles in custody. They have other stuff on him as well. Seems he likes to beat up photographers. Put his history, along with attempted kidnapping, assault, and it's not likely they'll let him walk."

"Lucky for him," Nick said evenly. "This is his last shot at Kate. They let him go and he will deal with me."

Nick dismissed the five of them and they scattered quickly. This was a nightmare scene of the worst kind. And seeing Kate, her hands and clothes drenched in Brock's blood, desperately trying to clamp off a slashed artery, was almost more than Nick's temper could stand. He usually kept his temper down, staying level tempered, even when he was past being mad. This was something he had worked very hard on for many years – it used to take very little to ignite it. But now, when Nick was mad, people knew it by the look on his face – he didn't have to yell at people. Today, however, was different. Two people were almost killed because of this and he'd let the whole group have the brunt of his temper.

Mike opened the door and stuck his head in. "Nick, there's someone here to see you."

"This probably isn't a good time, Mike," Nick answered, his tone icy.

"He says he's your brother," Mike continued, managing not to cringe. "I saw his identification and he at least has the same last name. He even looks like a grey haired version of you."

This was all he needed. Wonder what I did to irritate them this time – just being in the same city? "Let him in."

Nick stood and waited behind a long table. The door opened again and his brother, Trevor, walked into the room. "Nick," he said in greeting.

"Trevor, today is *not* a good day if you're here to start any kind of tirade," Nick said, not sounding very friendly. "Two of my people were almost killed last night; I've had no sleep, and I'm not in a fit mood to deal with much - especially your nonsense."

"I'm sorry to hear it," Trevor said, ignoring his last comment. "Are they all right?"

"My keyboard player is fine, physically – my security person is still in the hospital."

"Nick," he started again hesitantly, coming to stand in front of him. "I came to apologize for what happened after Dad's funeral." Nick stood there looking at him, not certain he was hearing him correctly. "I know a simple apology is not going to cover it, nor will it cover the other forty years of anger, but I saw the banners stating you were here. I thought I would come over and at least give it a shot."

"Why?" Nick asked pointedly. "And how the bloody hell did you know which hotel I was at?"

"Mind if I sit?" he asked, and Nick motioned him over to one of the overstuffed chairs in the room and sat down opposite him. "Mum told me you usually stay here at Claridge's or at the Millennium. The manager didn't want to admit you were here – but I guess my identification was convincing enough because he pointed me up to your security on the fifth floor. And the why – because I didn't think what Phillip did was right. After the funeral, he just grabbed my jacket and dragged me over to you – I had no idea he planned to slam you up against the wall. And I was shocked at what he said."

"It was definitely uncalled for," Nick said. "I know I bring a lot of attention when I show up places, but I'd always thought home was safe."

"Well, it's been eating at me ever since. I've no idea why he's always been so hard on you but it wasn't right," Trevor said, pausing for a moment. "I'm sorry for what happened. And I would be open to the thought of trying to build a better relationship between us."

"Damn," Nick said. "If someone had told me my brother would be here apologizing to me about anything, I'd have laughed in their face. I accept your apology, Trevor, but I'll have to think about the other. There have been far too many years to simply wash it away clean."

"I understand, Nick. I wanted you to know I was sincere."

The two men were interrupted when the door opened and Kate walked in. "I'm sorry, Nick," Kate started. "I didn't realize you had someone in here."

"It's fine," he assured her, trying to ignore the bandage on her neck. "How's Brock?"

"Better this morning," she said, smiling. "Doctor thinks they can release him in the morning."

"And he will be on the first plane home."

"I don't know he's going to go that easily, Nick," she said. "He knew you'd try to send him home. He said he'll be fine in a couple of days and he's staying."

"We'll see," was all Nick answered. "Come over here, love, there's someone I'd like you to meet."

Kate walked over and stopped short as the two men stood up. Nick smiled at her expression - he knew what she was thinking. He and Trevor looked identical, except Trevor's hair was gray and Nick was the taller of the two.

"Kate, this is my brother, Trevor," Nick said. "Kate is my keyboard player."

"I am pleased to meet you," Trevor said, putting his hand out for handshake. "Nick said there was an accident last night. You're all right?"

"I will be," Kate said, dodging the question, clearly not wanting to talk about it. "I've got to go finish moving my stuff out of my old room so the maids can clean up but I wanted to get a cup of coffee first. It's good to meet you."

Both men sat down as Kate left. "Pretty girl."

"Talented as hell, too. She trained to be a concert pianist once."

"Then what is she doing in a rock and roll band?" he asked.

"Funny you should ask,' Nick said grimly. "Ten years ago, her ex-husband pushed her down a flight of stairs and crushed her hand so she could no longer play concert pieces. Incidentally, he's the same guy who almost killed her last night."

"Sounds like you had quite a scene here."

"He got one of the maids to let him on the floor and he tried to kidnap her. Seems he's a bit unstable where she is concerned – he was ranting about how no one walks out on him, which she basically did. When one of my security people tried to intervene, they wrestled and the bastard stabbed him in the thigh. Kate closed off the artery to stop the blood, bleeding herself from the scratch she had gotten, and held the artery all the way to the hospital until the surgeons could get a clamp on it. She literally saved Brock's life with her own hands."

"There's something else," Trevor said gently. "There's something other than anger on your face. The way you feel about her is more than professional, and this scared you."

Nick looked sharply at him. "You've hardly said two words to me for the past twenty years and you can pick up on that when no one else has?"

"I don't see you day in and day out," Trevor answered. "So?"

"She is the essence of what's good in my life," Nick admitted on a sigh. "We were supposed to get married last week, but other things got in the way. And, until we get do, I have this crazy block which won't let me sleep with her while we're on tour. Right now I'm her employer and the idea smacks wrong. So to have this happen and I can't do much to comfort her, it's doing nothing to resolve my temper."

"You won't get any negative comments from me, Nick," Trevor said. "I'm glad you've found someone who makes you happy. I know the last go around with this didn't end on a good note and you've been alone a long time."

"No, it didn't," Nick agreed. "I never thought I would find someone else. Someone who could see past all the glitz and the fame."

"I have to go," Trevor said standing up. "I have classes this afternoon, so I need to get back. I just wanted to see you for a few minutes." Nick stood up and Trevor pulled him into a quick hug. "Go take care of your girl. Who gives a damn what anyone thinks."

Nick walked Trevor out to the elevator before making his way over to Kate's old room. The door was propped open and Nick stepped inside, coming to stand in the doorway to the bedroom. He watched while she put her clothes and things back into her suitcase; the maids usually did their unpacking. Last night, security had given her a new room so she wouldn't have to come back to this one. There were caution cones on the floor where Brock's blood had seeped into the carpet.

"How are you doing, love?"

"I'm good, Nick. Not an experience I would like to repeat," she answered, pausing in her efforts to look at him. "And I'm immensely thankful Brock took that moment to come into the sitting room for the night – I don't like what happened after though."

"I'm not too keen on it myself," Nick replied, closing the sitting room door and coming to stand next to her. He pulled her into his arms and his mouth found hers. There was a multitude of emotions coming through, but Kate didn't waver as she returned it. After the kiss, he continued to hold her to him. "I am still so angry. Scared *and* angry, actually."

"I had a few nightmares myself last night," she said. "You didn't sound very good at breakfast."

"It was taking all my will not to blow up until I got the band out of the room," he admitted. "Security will probably be a little scarce today if I'm around. I don't like yelling at people – I shouldn't have to and most of the time a look will get the point across. I wasn't very friendly to my brother either – every time one of them is around I'm always sure there's an agenda I won't like."

"What did he want?"

"He came to apologize for what happened after the funeral. I was almost floored when he said it, like a dream."

"Why do you suppose he did?"

"I have no idea. He said he didn't think what Phillip did was right. And, from the sound of things, Trevor was drawn into it without any knowledge of what Phillip had planned to do. He threw out the olive branch to try to start being friends."

"Big step."

"It is. I need to find out what he told my mum – it's how he found me here. She knows not to give out my locations when I'm touring, so he'd to have been pretty convincing for her to disclose that. And the fact he's my brother wouldn't have made a difference – she knows we're not close."

"I'm glad he made the effort. You seemed relaxed with him," she observed.

"It's a start. I told him I'd think about it," Nick said, pausing to look at the bandage on her neck. "Can I see how bad it is?"

"I was planning to take it off anyway before the show. Put a scarf over it if I need to," Kate said in confirmation.

Nick reached up and gently started to release the tape holding the gauze to her throat. He was going slow to not irritate the skin and he was inwardly holding his breath, preparing himself for what he was going to see. Once he pulled the gauze loose, the cut wasn't too bad – it looked much like a scratch from a cat's claw. It hadn't been very deep and appeared to have already started scabbing over.

"It doesn't look bad, love," Nick said, smiling to reassure her. "Looks like you and a cat got into it."

He watched as she stepped away from him to look in the bathroom mirror. "Still going to put a scarf over it. It feels much better with the tape off."

"I'll bet. I have to go call the studio and some other folks, then I might crash for a bit. You'll be all right?"

Kate nodded. "I'll be fine. I'm going to see about getting a car and going out to Stuarts." Stuarts was a London store who sold her brand of jeans. "Seems I am down a pair of jeans and a shirt," she said with a smile.

Nick kissed her again and ran his hand down her cheek. The terror was started to ease now he knew it wasn't more than a scratch and it was helping to drop his anger level. He opened the door and left, going to his room and planning to get a couple hours of sleep. The remainder of the day was quiet and the band left as normal for the Hall where they were playing the second of a three night stand. Nick was out in the hallway, smoking a cigarette when Sam came over and whispered into Nick's ear.

Nick swore under his breath, stubbing the cigarette out. He could sense his anger coming back, seeping back into him. Nick told Sam not to say anything until after the show; he would tell Kate that her ex-husband had committed suicide in his jail cell. Nick had no idea what this was going to do to Kate's mental frame of mind. She already felt bad about Brock – this could push her controlled emotion over the edge.

* * *

After the show, Nick took Kate's arm and motioned for her to go toward the big meeting room at the hotel. Sam followed and the three of them entered the room together. Kate knew something was up – Nick didn't usually interact with anyone after a show unless something was going on. And then it was usually one on one – so having Sam in the room did not bode well. Nick led her over to one of the over-stuffed chairs and Sam remained posted at the door to keep people out.

"Okay," Kate said. "What's going on?'"

"I have to tell you something and it's not going to be good," Nick started.

Kate's first thought was something had happened to one of her parents and she could feel the tension starting in her stomach. But she had been with Nick long enough to know she had to wait until he found the right words to tell her. "Whatever it is, Nick, give it to me straight. Don't try to wrap it up with a nice pink bow."

"Kevin Miles committed suicide this afternoon."

Kate was stunned. This was not what she was expecting and did not know what to say.

"And it gets worse, love. This is going to be all over the papers by morning and it's going to be a hell of a mess before it is done." Nick looked at her evenly. "Sam and the guys will keep the reporters off you as much as they can, but it's possible they will get to you the next time we leave. You need to be prepared for the onslaught."

"Suicide," she said softly. "I can barely believe it."

"The lead detective called Sam before the show. They found him hanging by his belt in the cell," Nick said, trying to keep his tone level. "Because he was only in a holding cell and not an actual jail cell, they didn't take away his belt, shoelaces or any other personal effects, other than his wallet. They also found a bunch of stuff in his apartment that indicates he's been stalking you for the past six months. The detectives went over this morning to his apartment looking for any substantiating evidence as to why he attacked you."

"Since New York."

"And I probably made it worse then, although I didn't mean to," Nick said explaining. "I called the director of the London symphony the next morning we were there, and basically told them to pull Miles back to London, so there wouldn't be a chance of any more encounters with him. I give lots of money to them as a charity donation - they didn't want to lose that."

"I knew he was angry I slipped away from him after the accident ten years ago," Kate said, in an introspective tone of voice. "He tried to see me when I was in the hospital, but my lawyer was able to get a restraining order until the divorce hearing. I dropped out of sight after they discharged me − I didn't use credit cards and paid cash for everything so I couldn't be traced." Kate smiled. "My lawyer even got me a fake ID with an address in Brooklyn so he would think I lived there. I would hate to think he stalked out the apartment building looking for me."

"Kate, love, this is a lot to absorb in a short amount of days. Are you sure you're all right?"

"I'm sure I will be," she answered honestly. "Am I going to go do something stupid, like disappear or hurt myself? The answer is no. To be honest with you, Nick, I'm actually relieved. This is hard but I know there's an ending and I don't have to keep looking around corners for him."

Nick motioned for Sam to leave. Sam opened the door and stepped out quietly. Nick stood up and pulled Kate up with him, putting his arms around her, holding her against him. "You can stay with me tonight," Nick said softly, "If you want."

Kate smiled, knowing she had been right -this broke the block. But she knew better than to act on it. "There is nothing I would like better; to lose myself in the warmth of your arms," she answered. "But I'm not going to give any kind of ammunition to the tabloids." She brought his head down to kiss her and the kiss seemed to go on forever before she broke off, stepping away from him and leaving the room.

In the morning, Sam brought copies of the morning paper along with a handful of tabloids. On the front of all of them was a photo-shopped picture of Kevin, brandishing a wicked looking knife and one headline was 'Crazed Musician on the Rampage'. Kate rolled her eyes when she saw it and had to give a lot of credit to Nick's security people. They had managed to keep her name out of the mess, although there were lots of references Kevin had attacked someone in Nick Marshall's backup band who happened to be in London for some performances.

"I don't know how this junk sells," Kate said to no one in particular.

"Sex and violence," Trent added. "Makes a story much more intriguing."

"How can intelligent people read this stuff?"

"That's the problem, love," Nick chimed in. "Most of them are *not* intelligent. They live hard, boring lives and think this is entertainment."

"I'm sorry to have brought it on," Kate said. "Last thing I wanted was an episode from my past creating news."

"Don't let it bother you, Kate," Andy said, coming over to put his hand on Kate's shoulder. "I'm sure Nick can find something to bump your issue off the front page with."

Nick threw one of the grapes from his plate at Andy and everyone started laughing. Kate knew Nick did his best to ignore what was written about him and made great strides to not do much in public so as not to fuel the fire. But it wasn't unusual to see some false tidbit about him.

CHAPTER TEN

After finishing up two weeks in Great Britain, the group moved on to Belgium, France and Italy. The first two countries were uneventful and put them at the halfway point when they got to Italy. Nick's music was immensely popular in Europe and it didn't matter the shows were all in English. The music lineup was different here, as Nick was not using his own concert equipment, instead paying to use whatever was available at each venue. The songs which were dependent on the regular piano were cut from the program and others put in its place. It was not a hardship for Kate since she could sight read and Nick had given her his music after she had signed the master contract. Everyone kept their instruments with them at the hotel and the road crew would set them up when they arrived in each city. European tours were a little more difficult because Nick flew everyone from city to city in a private jet. He had learned the hard way not to have a truck full of stage equipment trying to pass security checkpoints. More than once, he had equipment confiscated by greedy officials and that inconvenience was difficult to work through - usually ending with him having to buy more at ridiculously high prices to make the show each night.

It was a slow, rainy day in Naples, Italy. They had done a show the night before and there was another one tonight, before heading to Rome. Even though the weather was bad, the rest of the guys wanted to go sightseeing and had left after breakfast. Kate didn't like going out in the rain and opted to stay back. She was in the large sitting room they used as a general room, playing solitaire. She had the television on for noise, but the channels were limited and none she could find in English. She was enjoying the slow day and smiled at Sam when he came into the room. Sam was Nick's main security, usually not too far from wherever Nick was, and he also seemed to be a really nice guy. Most of Nick's security were large, imposing guys that normal people wouldn't want to mess with and Sam was no exception, standing at six-foot-five and weighing about three hundred pounds. He was definitely not someone you would want to meet on a dark night. During shows, security did a good job of keeping the fans off the stage. Four would stand along the seating floor and two toward the back on the stage; no one got past them onto the stage.

Sam poured a cup of coffee and sat down across from Kate, watching her play. She stopped after a few hands and looked him over. "Something bothering you, Sam?" she asked.

"What's going on with you and Nick?"

"Going on with what?" she asked, trying not to give anything away.

"Kate," he said, pointedly looking at her. "I know Nick better than anyone, next to Mickey. He has been a different person these past few months and the only thing which changed was you." Sam took a sip of his coffee, the cup seeming tiny in his hand. "Well, except for the tour we did last year. *It* was difficult because Marcus's wife kept harassing Marcus, saying she needed him at home. Nick does not deal well with strife. This is different."

"Is that why Marcus quit?" she asked, trying to divert him.

"Yes. Nick gave him a job as a studio musician so he could be home with his family more. They had one of those 'oops' babies, when theirs were almost grown, and his wife couldn't handle it. Nick doesn't use hired studio people – all of his people record and tour with him, so this spot was opened. But you're trying to change the subject."

No wonder Nick liked this security company so well. They had the same bulldog attitude Nick did about stuff. It wouldn't surprise her if Nick owned their company as part of the studio. "Maybe you should ask Nick."

"I thought I would start with you," Sam said. "At first, I thought you and Brock had started something. I'd never seen him be so protective before and I was a little worried - he has a solid marriage with a couple of kids. But it became apparent it wasn't what was happening so I started to watch in a different direction, especially after the events in London. Come on, spill it."

Kate didn't know whether she should just tell him. She didn't think that he would be indiscreet, but this was something she and Nick hadn't made a decision on. "Brock's a good guy. His lessons in self-defense were invaluable."

Kate paused for a moment, putting her words together. "Nick and I were supposed to get married during the break. Unfortunately the whole episode with Jamie Garwood kept Nick too busy."

"Married?" Sam asked, with an incredulous tone. "Nick proposed marriage?"

"You sound surprised."

"I don't know surprised even covers it," Sam answered. "Stunned is more like it. Nick has been saying for years he had no intention of *ever* getting married again."

"We fought it," Kate admitted. "It started after the fiasco with my ex in New York. You know, stolen moments, an occasional kiss when no one was around. We knew for sure when he got back from London, emotionally all torn up."

"Yeah, those few days were bad," Sam concurred. "I don't think I've ever seen him so messed up. I had to drag him back to the airport; he was so out of it."

"I'm glad you were there, Sam."

"You and me both. What escalated this," he motioned, waving his hand through the air between them, "to where he would even consider marriage?"

"I was sick when we finished the first tour. I passed out in the studio when we were recording the movie track and he took me back to his place to take care of me. He and his housekeeper were my lifeline for two full days - I still don't remember much of it. And, well, it just happened – we finally jumped the hurdle of he was my boss and we ended up in bed together. More information than you were probably looking for... I'd appreciate it if you didn't tell anyone else that."

"I won't," he said. "But now I'm going to ask the big question. Why aren't you guys sleeping together now?"

Kate had the grace to blush. "Nick's concerned about what the rest of the band would think. He sees it as no different as a boss bedding his secretary. It's frustrating, I'll admit. And if Nick has been more terse lately, it's probably why."

Sam started to smile. "Now, *that* sounds like Nick. And Kate –sorry if I was being too nosy."

"It's okay, Sam. I know you're out to protect him."

"It's not a bad thing," he assured her. "Nick has grown hard, distant, over the years and it's nice to see him starting to relax some. Don't worry, Kate. I won't say anything."

* * *

Sam smiled as he got up and left the room. He wanted to dance in the hall because Nick wanting to get married was like something out of a fairy tale. And he wasn't about to let this get away because of a lack of time. He had a wild idea of something to do when they got to Rome but he had to confirm what Kate had been saying. Sam knew Nick was in his room on the phone with the studio, so he thought he would go relieve Mike and wait for the opportunity to talk to him. Mike was happy to be free to eat, and maybe see some sights, so he was out the door in a flash. Sam picked up a magazine on the end table to occupy his time until Nick got off the phone.

Sam coming in and relieving Mike didn't disturb Nick. He never looked up. Security went in and out of rooms with him all the time. Sam was beginning to think Nick was glued to the phone more than he used to be. He knew that Nick made a lot of changes since buying into the studio, but the excessive amount of phone calls he was having to absorb had to be messing with his patience.

Once off the phone, Nick stood up, stretching his muscles. Sam saw he was finished and set the magazine back on the table. He got up and stood in the doorway. "Hey, Nick?"

"Yeah, Sam?"

"Can I ask you a straight question?"

"Sure, mate," he said. "What's on your mind?"

"Do you and Kate have something going on?"

Nick was harder to read than Kate, but he saw the flicker in his eyes. "What makes you think we have something going on?"

Slouching against the door frame, Sam started to laugh. "Nick, I've known you almost twenty years. I can *smell* when something is different. And the only change has been Kate."

"It's a mess, Sam," Nick admitted. "I told myself when I hired her, I wouldn't touch her. But I just can't help myself."

"How does she feel about you?"

"What are you, my therapist?" Nick asked. Sam kept smiling at him, his gaze never wavering, not at all affected by Nick's cynical tone. "I want to marry her, Sam. And I would have during the break, if that bloody Jamie Garwood had kept it in his pants."

"I have an idea how to fix this tomorrow - let me make some phone calls. By the way," he asked curiously, "do you have a ring?"

Nick started to laugh. "Yes, I have a ring. But what makes you think anything needs fixing?"

"I have been watching you both and it's obvious neither of you are happy," Sam stated. "Oh, and make sure you bring the ring with you tomorrow night. You'll need it."

* * *

Sam left the room, apparently to go make his 'calls.' Nick shook his head as the phone rang yet again and, sitting back down in the chair, he answered it. It was the studio, of course, but this time it was just a couple of the PR folks in London with some questions. Those kinds of calls tended to take much less time. Once off that call, he started thinking about what Sam had been saying. He had no idea what he was planning, but it didn't surprise him Sam had seen straight through the façade he and Kate had tried to build. And, if he had a way to expedite his marriage to Kate, Nick was all for it. He pulled the ring out of his pocket, looking at the way the diamond in the middle sparkled. He had brought it for no other reason than he liked what it represented.

His nerves had settled down since London. Suicide wasn't exactly what he had been hoping for as a resolution for Kate's ex, but he was glad that page in her history was done. And somehow they had managed to keep it low key in the press, because, after the initial morning of tabloid headlines, the story died down quickly. Also, the whole boss-employee thing had disintegrated but Kate had remained steadfast – she could have accepted his offer that night but had flat turned him down with no change in the six weeks which followed. Nick had mixed feelings about it – so he was glad Sam was going to put something together.

* * *

During break in the show in Rome, Sam found Kate as she was coming back from the ladies room. "When this is done tonight, make sure you get in the front car with Nick."

Kate had no idea why he was so adamant but nodded her agreement anyway and got ready for the next half of the show. Nick did all his ballads in the first half so the second was hard rock and roll music and it was a lot more demanding. Nick usually did one encore – two if he was feeling really good, and as soon as they were done, Sam whisked Kate and Nick into the front car along with himself and the driver. The four of them drove off into the Italian landscape. And this was making Kate nervous - she had no idea what was going on. She had originally thought Nick's security was trying to defuse some issue and wanted them out of the way quickly. The thought disappeared as they drove quietly through the countryside until they reached what looked like an old church. It was set upon a mountain top and in the daylight, Kate was sure you could see down into the city of Rome. At night though, it was dark with very little light in the courtyard. Sam opened the door for Kate and led the couple into the church proper.

"What's going on Sam?" Kate asked.

"Well, I am here to fix what didn't happen before we left LA," Sam said, with a smile. "This is where I married my wife ten years ago."

That was news to Kate; she had no idea Sam even had a wife. "And?"

There was a priest at the end of the pews toward the altar. "Father Giovanni is here to marry you two."

"Marry us?" Kate sputtered. "Sam, this is craziness. I'm not Catholic."

"Neither is he," Sam said smiling. "This is a Greek Orthodox church."

Nick started to laugh. "You're something, mate," he said. "I'd no idea this is what you were planning."

"This is only the first part," Sam answered mysteriously. "So let's do this before you guys get cold feet."

Sam herded them into the church and marched them down the aisle together. As Father Giovanni started his blessing, in English no less, Kate started to realize that this was truly happening. Nick hadn't said much but had a tight hold of her hand.

The whole thing felt like a dream, with the priest going through the ceremony. She repeated her vows with a steady voice and was surprised when Nick pulled a diamond band out of his pocket. It had an upraised diamond in the center with smaller diamonds going down each side; the ring was small, dainty, and not bulky. Nick slid it on Kate's finger, fitting perfectly, and the priest finished his blessing. As soon as he was done, Nick kissed Kate. They thanked the priest and Sam hurried them back into the car.

"What's the rush, mate," Nick asked. "You act like you are on a deadline."

"It's already past midnight so you don't have much time before morning."

* * *

They drove only a few minutes before pulling up in front of a gorgeous house. There was a sign stating it was a bed and breakfast, and Nick quickly figured out the second part of Sam's plan. It touched him Sam had gone to so much effort. The evening had been surreal – Nick could hardly believe they had gotten married. It was not something he had been actively working on. He and Kate had discussed maybe going to Las Vegas after this tour finished, but it had been purely speculation. Based on the rules Nick had set in place, they didn't get much face time together and Kate was still holding to his edict, even though it was no longer an issue. When the car stopped, Sam got out and went inside. He was back with a room key in mere moments.

"Okay, guys. Top floor, room seven," he said. "I'll be back to get you in the morning, say around eleven?"

Nick took the key and held his hand out to Sam. Sam took it and Nick pulled him into a quick hug. "I owe you, mate," he said, releasing him.

"Hey, not a problem. I figured I better act while the irons were hot. Didn't want either of you changing your mind."

Sam got into the car and it drove off into the night. Nick was surprised Sam left them there, no security lagging behind, but he had seemed to know the place well. He took Kate's hand and led her inside. The staircase was to the right and they walked the two flights up to a door with the number seven on it. Nick unlocked the door, standing to the side to allow Kate to enter first. The room was decorated in white lace and there was a king sized bed in the middle. Nick smiled, locking the door behind them. It was dimly lit but there was more than enough light to see by.

"Come here," Nick said, as Kate moved into his arms. "This has been so incredible."

"Not what I expected when Sam told me to make sure I got into the front car. I thought there was something going on."

"Well there was, love," he answered, teasing her. "Just not what you were thinking."

"No, not what I was thinking. And you even had a ring – makes me wonder if you weren't behind it."

"Hey, this was all Sam," he said, hugging her tighter. "I bought the ring in LA, before the whole Garwood fiasco. I brought it with me because I liked what it meant - even kept it in my pocket for good luck. "

"Are you sure this is what you really want, Nick?" Kate asked, in a serious tone. "I know you haven't been a big fan of marriage and how binding it is. It's not too late to undo this."

"I have never been more certain of anything in my life," Nick said softly, his lips touching hers. "But the big question is whether or not you are, Kate. You know being married to me is going to be difficult. I'm not a romantic, in any sense of the word, and I don't know much about sharing. I only know I love you."

"And I love you enough to want to make it work," Kate answered, pulling his head down to hers, deepening the kiss. Nick made a noise in his throat before scooping her up in his arms and placing her on the bed, lying down beside her.

* * *

Sam was back at exactly eleven the next morning. He and the driver pulled in front of the house to find Nick and Kate waiting for him, sitting on the front steps. Sam took a minute to look them over; he was sure he hadn't seen Nick so relaxed in ages. Nick had his arm wrapped around Kate's knee, holding her to him and his head was bent, listening to what she was saying. His hair fell between them like a light cloud, as he had left it loose. That, more than anything, told Sam he was relaxed - the only time he ever left it down was on stage or as he was going to bed. Nick stood up as Sam got out of the car and he reached down to help pull Kate to her feet. Kate was smiling too and it made Sam feel good that he had made the right decision.

"Looks like you two had a good night," Sam observed, as they got into the back seat of the car.

"It was very good," Nick confirmed and smiled, watching Kate as she blushed a little at his comment.

"You didn't miss much. Only one of the light booms falling and breaking two lights."

"You're serious?" Nick asked. "Are they fixable?"

"Your crew is working on it," Sam confirmed. "Mickey sounded confident when he was telling me earlier this morning."

"It's always something, mate. Someday I'd like to get through just one tour without something breaking."

"That's why you have insurance," Sam reminded him.

"Oh I know," Nick said. "I'm not sure which is worse: the cost of the insurance or the equipment – it's about the same."

"Here," Sam said, handing an official looking paper to Kate. It was an off-white color and was written in Italian. The only thing Kate recognized was her name and Nick's, and it was stamped with an upraised mark. "What's this?"

"It's your marriage certificate," he told her. "You'll need it to change your name."

"I'm not changing my name."

"Did you know that?" Sam asked Nick.

"I knew," Nick confirmed. "She wants to stand on her own two feet professionally. And, personally, I think it's a good idea. It will keep things out of the press longer; the less people know and all that."

"I'll buy that," Sam agreed. "I've been surprised the tabloids haven't been making much of Kate being the only woman in your band."

"Well, let's just say money talks," Nick answered, mysteriously.

"What does that mean?" Sam asked.

"The American papers are too busy with other tidbits to chase after me. The British ones I paid off to kill any story."

"And they agreed?"

"All right, there were some threats of a lawsuit over what happened when my dad passed, when they were out trying to get a story at the house. The agreement to drop the lawsuit, and a few extra dollars, kept the story basically dead," Nick answered confidently. "Everything is ready for the flight tomorrow to Tokyo?" Nick asked, changing the subject.

"As far as I know. Mickey said we all need to be at the airport by six."

The car pulled up at the hotel and the three of them got out and went inside. Sam whispered something to Nick and he smiled, taking Kate's hand in his as they got up to the floor. Keeping a hold of her hand, Nick followed Sam into the general room and all kinds of cheers went up. The other guys had done some quick decorating and there was food, champagne, and a big cake on the table at the back of the room. Nick and Kate were crushed by a wall of well-wishers – all the guys seemed exceptional happy at what had taken place.

CHAPTER ELEVEN

The months after the European tour had ended were trying for both Nick and Kate. Nick dove into his job at the studio but it was apparent the lack of planning and leadership which was in place was going to more than try his patience. Jerry's general manager had quit while Nick was on the road and the remaining managers were trying to keep things running without any direction. Nick came back to chaos at its best and it was taking a toll on their still-new marriage. In between working to get things back to normal, Nick was also trying to get the rest of the songs written for his next record album and it was going very badly as he didn't have the time nor the solitude he needed to get it done. Kate, thankfully, was not a needy person, and she had left him alone while he tried to work out his frustrations with his music. Most nights Kate went to bed long before Nick slid in beside her. Sometimes days would go by and the only way she knew he was still there was he usually woke her up when he came to bed. Kate never said anything but would watch him as he quietly undressed and got into bed. Nick was getting a lot of headaches and if something didn't get resolved soon, the stress was likely to give him a heart attack.

Kate came out of the bathroom on Friday night and was surprised to find Nick sitting on his side of the bed, partially undressed for bed and smoking a cigarette. He smiled when she walked in the room, but she could see it was superficial at best. She slipped her robe off and climbed on the bed behind him. He stiffened when she pushed the shirt off his shoulders, thinking she was wanting his intentions in bed. She could see he was in no mood for it; she was sure he had a terrific headache. Instead, she started massaging his back, just below the shoulder blades. She pushed out more than one big knot in his muscles before moving to the tops of his shoulders, along the base of his neck. She felt him relax, leaning back against her as her sure fingers kept working out his tension. Ever so gently, she started up the sides of his face. She had learned this when her father was sick - it helped him relax enough for the pain medication to kick in. And it was doing wonders for Nick. He moved only to put out the finished cigarette in the ash tray but was a prisoner to Kate's touch. He was almost asleep sitting up when she finished.

"Kate," he started, but she put her hand over his mouth.

"SSH," was all she said. She pushed him down on the bed and reached over to turn off the lamp on his side of the bed. She pulled the covers over on him and lay on his chest. "Sleep," she told him quietly. "We'll talk tomorrow."

Nick nodded and wrapped his arm around her in response, asleep in just a few minutes. Kate laid awake for a little while, listening to his even breathing. She didn't have all the answers but had a few ideas she had been working on to help. It had taken her some time to notice the toll the stress was taking on him since she had been working hard herself. The studio manager had been ecstatic to have her talents and found her more than enough work to keep her busy. But it wasn't like Nick to be so distant with her and she had noticed it getting worse in the last month or so.

In the morning, Nick was out of bed before she woke, but listening to the quiet house, she could hear the light sounds of an acoustic guitar. It was Saturday morning; Nick didn't normally work weekends and she wasn't currently working on any session. She pulled her robe on and went down into the kitchen. Starting the coffee, she pulled two mugs out of the cupboard. She went to the fridge, got out the milk, and poured some into the bottom of one of the mugs before adding sugar to both. Then once the coffee was done brewing, she quickly poured each mug and headed to the back of the house where Nick had his music room. Inside was a huge piano, a few folding chairs, and simple desk near where she found Nick sitting, strumming an old guitar and adding notes to the near empty sheet music in front of him. She set his cup of coffee down on the desk, away from the music, and sat down in one of the chairs across from him.

Nick put the guitar on the stand and set the pencil down, picking up the mug. "That smells heavenly," he commented.

"I thought you might like a cup. I was hoping we could talk for a little bit."

"It's a nice distraction," he answered. "That was the best sleep I've had in weeks, love."

"You can't go on the way you are, Nick. You're going to have a stroke or worse."

"I'm certainly learning I'm not an executive," he agreed, nodding. "I'm starting to wonder if it was a good idea to buy out half the studio."

"I don't think it was a bad investment," Kate said. "I just think you need to get a good general manager in there to pick up and run things."

"I've been looking, love. Haven't found anyone I really think could do the job. And they need to be able to do it without my looking over their shoulder every five minutes."

"I have an idea to run by you."

"I'm listening."

"Why don't you get Mickey back here to get things straightened up until you can hire a manager?" Kate asked. "Mickey's a walking planning machine and organized chaos seems to be his specialty."

"He's on tour with the new band he's been promoting, At Last," Nick told her. "Somewhere in Colorado right now, I think."

"Bet you could still get him back. He's only managing small groups because he's waiting for you to get ready to start touring again. You're normally his full time job."

"It won't be this year if I don't start making headway. I only have about five songs completed. I can usually write a song in about a week or three. It's taken me since we got back from Europe to write what I have."

"I also think you need to buy Jerry out," Kate continued, with a definite tone. "I believe he's a major part of your frustrations."

"I've been thinking the same thing. Every time I think I have something solid working, he goes along behind me and changes it," he confirmed. "I'm sure we don't have what it takes to be partners."

"Will he sell to you?" Kate asked.

"Might... if the price is right. He's been talking about wanting to retire at some point and travel. Maybe I can get him to agree to something."

"At least you could do things your way," she said. "You wouldn't have someone changing stuff when you weren't looking."

"True," he agreed. He looked at her and smiled. "I'm really sorry, love. I know I've been a right bastard to you lately."

"I never expected every day to be roses with you, Nick. Marriage is give and take and we're still really new at it. Neither of us had a lot of experience with marriage, or long relationships for that matter."

"No, we haven't. But I need to learn not to shut you out. That's a new concept for me."

"I only want to add to your strength. That's why I've left you alone to deal with things."

"I think your idea of calling Mickey might be a good one," Nick said pensively, clearly chewing the idea over in his head. "At least help me get a good framework in place while I keep looking."

"And I would also sit down with Jerry and tell him what you are doing. Hopefully he will respect that and let you run with it. He tasked you with the daily running of things – he should stay out of it."

"I'll start talking to my attorneys about buying him out. I think you are spot on with that also."

Kate stood, picking up her now empty coffee cup. "I'll leave you to your work. I didn't want to not say anything this morning."

"What were you planning to do today? Do you have to go into the studio?"

She shook her head. "No, I finished with the end of the keyboard tracks I was doing. It's all vocals now."

"Let's go do something, love," he prompted. "Maybe go for a drive to Santa Barbara."

"You're sure? You won't get any work done that way."

"It'll be here when I get back. I'd like to spend a quiet day with my wife."

"I'm going to go take a shower. Then I can be ready pretty quickly."

"I'll finish this verse and meet you at the door."

Kate smiled and walked out of the room. Nick turned back to the guitar, picking it up and going back to where he had left off. He knew his lack of creativity was a product of the stress he was enduring and was actually looking forward to spending the day with Kate. He knew of a restaurant along the coast which was quiet and out of the way. His hair wasn't its normal long length and he found that he wasn't being recognized quite as much as when it was flowing down his back. A ball cap and his sunglasses should take care of the rest.

Nick's car had a sunroof and he opened it while they drove up the coast. The weather was beautiful and the conversation was animated between them as they enjoyed the scenery. Almost to Santa Barbara, Nick pulled off at one of the beach parks and they got out, kicking their shoes off as they started walking on the sand to the water, hand in hand. The water was warm as it lapped at their ankles. Kate began kicking the water toward Nick. In turn, he started to chase her and she tried to evade him, both of them landing in the sand, laughing, as he caught her. The look of love was back in his eyes – the look she had been missing for the past couple of months.

* * *

Nick called Mickey once they got back. He agreed to come back and help Nick put some kind of structure in place at the studio. His new band was done with their mini-tour so it was a good time for him. Nick also did some research and came up with an offer to Jerry for the rest of the studio, which he rejected as he didn't think it was high enough. Jerry countered with a number making Nick swear loud enough in his office to make his secretary, Terry, blush. But Nick wasn't going to give up – and he had his people make a larger offer - one Jerry agreed to. Once the dust settled, Nick would be the sole owner of Empire Records on April first. And, with Mickey running the daily stuff, Nick had been able to get the rest of his music written and sent off for the arrangement work to be done. Now all he had to do was find a manager to run the place, since Mickey would be traveling with the band once they started touring again.

Nick found early on it was easier to have Mickey on the road with him than to have to find him if something went astray. Three things he had learned toward the beginning of his career – drag his manager on the road with him, hire the same security each time, and record and tour with the same band members. The first kept all kinds of surprises from being an impediment; the second, you knew who the security guys were, their quirks and they knew yours; and lastly, the music didn't have to be learned by more than one set of musicians and what the fans got on stage was pretty close to what they heard on the record. Nick's shows were always sold out and, if there was time in the schedule, it wasn't unusual to have another night added, which always sold out as soon as it was advertised. Nick would do promotional spots on the local radio stations and that brought out fans in droves.

* * *

Nick had barely sat down behind his desk when Terry poked her head into his office. She was a no-nonsense person he had been lucky to find when he first bought out half the studio. She was in her late fifties and was very protective over Nick. *No one* got past her either on foot or on the phone.

"Nick," she said. "Michael Grayson is on line one for you."

Nick glanced at the clock on his desk. "It's barely seven thirty. What makes him think I would bloody be here this early?"

Terry laughed, shaking her head. "Everyone knows you are a workaholic, Nick. I'm going down to personnel and will be back. I have Judy watching the door."

Nick picked up the receiver and pressed the flashing light that was line one. "Marshall."

"Hey, Nick," Michael Grayson answered. "How's it going?"

"Very well, I must say. I took full ownership of the studio this week," Nick answered.

"So I hear. All Jerry has been talking about is his retirement and where he wants to go."

"It was time," Nick said. "What can I do for you, mate?"

"Well, I have a small problem. One of my studio guys was in a car accident over the weekend and that puts me short a keyboard player," Michael said, pausing for a moment. "I'm wondering if there's any possibility I could borrow Kate Thomas for a couple of weeks?"

"Maybe," Nick said. "You'll have to talk to her. She keeps her own schedule."

"I thought I had to ask you first."

"You did," Nick answered. "But all my people work their own schedules when I don't have anything in the works. She takes the jobs she wants to do unless I am recording or touring, which will be next after I hire a manager to run this place."

"I have some ideas on that too, Nick, if you want to sit down and have lunch later this week."

"Works for me. Call Terry and schedule something on my calendar before it's all filled up. And I'll have Kate give you a call."

Nick finished the call and decided to go in search of his wife. It was weird sometimes, thinking of her that way, but in the year and a half since they were wed in Italy, only a few people knew they were actually married. Their professional relationship had stayed relatively the same, except that they shared the same suite now when Nick was touring and the guys knew the truth; they all approved enthusiastically. Kate had been adamant she still wanted to work and did not want Nick paying her way for everything. Their compromise had been he would continue to pay her like any other studio person and when they were on tour, which was workable when Nick only owned half the studio. Now that he was taking full ownership, it might not make sense. But it would be something he would have to discuss with Kate.

He went down to studio three where he knew she'd been working on an album for one of their artists. This one was being rushed so it would be available in the stores when the artist went on tour in a couple months. It made the sales much more lucrative if the new album was new in the stores when the show hit that city. Nick walked into the sound booth and smiled when he saw Kate. Kate was a gift – both musically and personally. Nick knew Grayson wanted her because she could sight read and it would keep whatever sessions planned on schedule. Kate grinned back at him, grabbed her water bottle, and made her way out of the studio into the booth. Nick walked back out into the hallway and Kate followed.

"What's up?" she asked.

"I had an early morning call from your previous employer."

"What did Michael want?" she asked.

"He was asking if he could borrow you to help finish an album. It seems one of his keyboard players was in a car accident."

"And your answer was?" she asked.

"I told him to ask you, love," Nick replied. "I wanted to tell him I wasn't your scheduling boy, but I didn't think he has the sense of humor to handle it very well."

Kate laughed. "I love your diplomacy, Nick. I'll call him and find out," she answered, giving him a quick hug before walking back into the studio.

When Nick got home, he found Kate in the kitchen making dinner. The same year and a half spent with Consuelo gave her all kinds of dinner ideas and it had manifested into some absolutely delicious meals. Nick came up behind her, wrapping his arms around her waist.

"Hello, love," he said, kissing her neck.

Kate leaned into him. "Some days I don't like my job, Nick."

"Then quit," he said. "Only work for me."

"I can't do that. I can't just sit around and drink lattes with the other non-working women. I called Michael."

"And?"

"He thinks you're a bad influence," she giggled. "He kept trying to tell me I made the wrong decision to come work for you. But he didn't even hesitate when I quoted him a figure about three times more than what I used to make over there."

"Serves him right. What about that son of his? Thought he could play keyboards."

"I know Michael lets Justin on some records. This one's out of his league, though. This is for Barry Ramsey."

Barry Ramsey was a highly known contemporary singer. He was in his mid-sixties and had a successful career on Broadway and when lounge singers were all the rage. His music was soft and electronic keyboards would not have been a good fit. "So you're going to work for the competition?"

"Hey, you said I could."

"I know, love," he said, turning her around to face him. "Sometimes I just want you all to myself."

His lips met hers and for a moment the here and now dropped away. Their chemistry was always that way – it was like a fairy tale come true. Kate broke off, turning back to what she had cooking on the stove. "You're incorrigible, Nick," she said.

"I know," he answered smiling. "After this, don't take anything else for a while. Trent should be done with this session's worth of classes in the next three weeks." Trent was going to Harvard to get his MBA during the breaks with Nick.

"Are you planning to put Trent to work when he gets finished?"

"Absolutely. Been saving the number three spot for him and he knows it too. Best of both worlds – gets a corporate job along with keeping his job as my drummer, which he said he wasn't looking to leave."

"You have all your music ready to go?" Kate asked.

"The arrangements came in today via FedEx," Nick answered. "I am anxious to go do something with it. All this office stuff is starting to make me climb the walls."

"What about the manager problem? If you don't find someone to run this, you'll spend all your spare time on the phone instead of most of it," she said, teasing him.

"Grayson mentioned he might have a solution. I'm supposed to find out what over lunch at the Foxwood Club on Wednesday."

"I'm pretty sure I know what he has in mind," she said.

"What might that be, love?"

"Michael's been grooming his eldest son, David. I'll bet he's ready to put him in place but it leaves the issue of the general manager he already has, Arlan Reynolds."

"How well do you know Arlan?" he asked.

"Pretty well. He ran the studio over there with a tight fist," she answered.

"Think he would be the right solution?"

"I do. He's no nonsense and is not afraid of long hours or extra work days. He would definitely keep you off the phone on the next tour. Or at least cut a good amount down."

"That's what I need," Nick agreed. "Hopefully it's something which will work out, because I can't do another year trying to run this."

CHAPTER TWELVE

Nick went to his lunch meeting with anxious feelings. *It would be bloody nice to have someone that could run this without a lot of interference from me*, he thought. Walking to the front door of the Foxwood Club, he was reminded again how blessed he was to have Kate for a wife. She had shown up about thirty minutes before he was going to leave with a jacket and a tie which matched the shirt and pants he had gone to work in. He was surprised to see her - he knew she was over at Satellite working on Barry Ramsey's record. Kate had laughed at him and told him she knew he wouldn't have been prepared. He scoffed at her but let her "dress him up" as it was, tying his tie and making sure everything was a good fit. As he continued to the entrance, all the men around him were in three piece suits and a few in a casual jacket and tie. He laughed to himself when he saw the sign at the front which read *'jacket and tie required'*. He would have to find out how she knew.

Michael Grayson was already there and stood as the hostess brought Nick over to his table. They shook hands and sat down. Michael had a good fifteen years on Nick – his dress and demeanor resembled his brother, Trevor. He was every inch the executive from the pinstriped suit to the diamond tie pin. They were day and night together; no one would believe Nick owned the second largest record company in the world – not with his hair starting to reach his shoulders and his casual appearance.

"Glad you could make it, Nick. This has been on my mind awhile," Michael started.

"I need the help," he admitted honestly. "I may own the company but, bottom line, I'm a musician. This last year has been bloody claustrophobic."

Michael laughed. "I could see where being desk bound could get old quick. In my case, it's all I have ever done."

"This is a nice place," Nick commented, looking around.

"I'm surprised you're not a member. You most certainly fit the qualifications."

Nick smiled. "It's not my thing, mate. Last time I put on a jacket and tie was at my father's funeral almost two years ago, and I had to borrow both from his closet. I can't remember past that. "

"Here's my dilemma," Michael started, wasting no time with preamble. "I've wanted my business to remain a family business. I have little to no interest in going public."

Nick nodded. He had the same sentiments about Empire.

"So my oldest son, David, has been learning the business since he got out of college. And I think he's ready to come in and take over as my general manager. But doing so leaves me with the one I currently have. Arlan Reynolds has been with me for over twenty years. I don't feel right dumping him out of a job. I'm hoping I can talk you into hiring him over at Empire."

"Have you talked to him about this?" Nick asked.

"Not specifically. I wanted to get your thoughts first. I know he's thinking he's on borrowed time."

"I need someone who can run the day to day operation with little or no input from me. I want to be back out on the road most of the time," Nick explained. "I want to handle the big stuff - who I sign, financial decisions, that sort of thing. My last road tour I was on the phone more than I was on stage."

"Arlan is your man, then. He could easily run my business on his own, except I *want* to be involved with the day to day stuff," Michael told him. He pulled a folder off the chair next to him. "Here's a copy of his personnel file; the last two yearly evaluations, pay scale, and an information sheet."

Nick took the file, setting it on the table beside him. "I'll go through it this week and let you know. I want to get on this quickly as I'm wanting to get back into the studio. Having to run everything has also cut down on my songwriting time. I get extremely irritated when I don't get to put my time where I really want to. I'm starting to drive my folks a little crazy."

"On the subject of studio time, thank you for letting me use Kate," Michael said. "Barry loves her."

"You're welcome, mate. If she has the time open, use her as much as you want. She has her own schedule."

Michael looked at him. "You have a pretty open mind, Nick. I don't know I'd have let her work for you when she was working for me."

"I don't own the woman, Michael. It would be detrimental for me to even try and I enjoy my free time." Michael had a confused look on his face and Nick couldn't help but laugh. "I'm sorry, mate. I forget sometimes not everyone knows. Kate's my wife."

"Wife? But she goes by Kate Thomas."

"Her idea. She doesn't want to get jobs because my name is attached to hers," Nick told him. "And she's not going to sit back and do nothing simply because she's married to me. She's a bigger work machine than I am. We've been married almost a year and a half."

"You didn't waste any time."

Nick smiled. "To tell you the truth, I fell head over heels in love with her. I'd pretty much given up on marriage after twenty years. And then boom."

"And I thought I knew everything happening in the music world," Michael mused. "I sure didn't see that coming."

"I didn't see it coming either, mate," Nick answered laughing. "And, in the beginning, I started with the ideals I would only see her as an employee. Some crazy things happened and they turned my thoughts around."

"You know her history?" Michael asked.

Nick nodded. "I know it. I also got to see the ending when her bastard ex-husband tried to kidnap her at knife point out of a London hotel."

"Okay, I really need to get out more. It isn't common knowledge either, is it?"

"We did our best to keep it hushed up in the press," Nick told him. "Her ex ended up committing suicide in his jail cell after he was arrested. Which suited me just fine because I was going to beat the bloody hell out of him once he got out of jail."

Michael chuckled. "Sounds like the right thing to me. She was a mess when I got her. I didn't need another keyboard player at the time but her dad is a good friend of mine. She turned out to be one of my best investments until you got a hold of her."

"Hey – I didn't go recruiting. She auditioned like everyone else," Nick said, holding his hands up, defending himself.

"True, you didn't," Michael agreed. "Still smarts though."

Nick laughed with him and the waiter brought over their lunch. The rest of the time was spent talking about other facets of the music business and some of the events each had attended. Michael complemented him on his Academy award nomination last winter for best song from the James Bond movie, although Nick didn't win. It was still a big deal to be nominated.

After lunch, Nick went through the folder of information and was back on the phone with Michael before the afternoon was done. Nick wanted to talk to Arlan – see if this was something he would want to take on. Based on evaluations, and what Kate had told him, he was interested. He told Michael he had an offer he wanted to make and Michael agreed to set up a meeting there at Satellite so Nick could meet with him. Knowing they both wanted to do this quickly, Michael set up the interview for Friday morning – two days after the lunch.

* * *

Nick was escorted into Michael's office by his secretary. Michael was behind the big oak desk that encompassed most of the room and there was another man sitting in one of the chairs in front of it. Michael made the introductions and Arlan stood to shake Nick's hand. Afterward, Michael left Nick alone with Arlan. Nick liked what he saw on the outside. Arlan was equally his height but had the build of a linebacker. He seemed only a little nervous which pleased Nick. He didn't want anyone who would be star struck over him. Having run this place for twenty years, he wouldn't expect that behavior, but one never knew.

"It is good to meet you, Nick," Arlan said, as they sat down. "My kids love your records."

Nick smiled. "So you're not a fan?"

Arlan smiled back, shaking his head. "Sorry. I'm country all the way." Nick could see that Arlan was confused as to why he was there. For Nick, it was like walking into the enemy camp.

"That's okay, mate," Nick answered. "I won't hold it against you. Did Michael tell you what his long-term plans are here at the studio?"

"He wants to give my job to his son. But then it has been his plan since I've been here."

"He also doesn't want to send you away with a pink slip," Nick told him. "That's where I come in. I want you to work for me at Empire."

Arlan was obviously surprised. "You're serious?"

"Absolutely. I need someone to run the place — the day to day operation. I'm a musician, not an administrator, and the last year of being one has reminded me smartly of that fact."

"You seem to have a lot of faith in me," Arlan said.

"I've done my homework and I won't lie to you, mate. Your workload will more than double what you do now, because I want no part of the daily work, which Michael is well involved with here. I want to go back to recording my records and going out on the road with my band. And in the interim, make the big decisions. So I need someone to run the place and I'm willing to pay for it."

Nick handed him a folded piece of paper. In it was a salary offer, along with quarterly bonus figures. Arlan's eyes widened when he saw the figure, which was more than double what he was currently earning, not counting the bonuses. "This is way too much, Nick."

"I guarantee you'll earn it. Here is how I see things," Nick answered seriously. "This will put you the number two man in charge, answering only to me. You will have full autonomy to run things as you see fit, within reason, of course. Hiring, firing, scheduling; anything which has to do with the daily running of things. The only exception to this is I have five musicians on the studio payroll who are contracted to me personally and, unless I'm recording or on the road, they're free to come ask you for work. You just can't put them in any kind of rotation or planning schedule."

"I can handle it," he answered. "Is Kate Thomas one of those?"

"She's my keyboard player," Nick answered, smiling. "And my wife."

"She seemed much happier when she came in to work on Barry Ramsey's album," Arlan told him. "I understand why now."

"So do we have a deal, mate?" Nick asked, standing up and holding out his hand.

Arlan stood up and took his hand in a firm handshake. "We do indeed. When do you want me to start?"

"I'll get the contract drawn up and whenever Michael is good to let you go, I'm ready. I want to get into the studio yet this year and go out on the road before the holidays, so the sooner the better."

* * *

Nick and Arlan walked out of Michael's office and rode the elevator down to the lobby. As they stepped off, Nick smiled when he saw Kate walking toward him with an older grey haired man which, as he got closer, he recognized as Barry Ramsey. Kate was all smiles walking up to the two men, Ramsey in tow.

"Nick, what are you doing here?" she asked.

"Hiring me a manager, love," he answered. "Arlan's coming to work for me."

"That's awesome," Kate said, giving Arlan a hug. Then she turned back to the older man. "Barry, I'd like you to meet my husband, Nick Marshall. Nick, this is Barry Ramsey."

The two men shook hands. "Wasn't expecting this," Barry said, shaking his head. "When you said you were married, Kate, I expected some suit and tie 'Mr. Thomas' to show up."

"Kate doesn't want my name interfering with her reputation," Nick answered. "But it's good to meet you. "

"And you. Thank you for loaning me Kate, the last songs seemed to just zip right by. I got more done this week with her than I had the past two months."

"Kate's the one you need to thank. She agreed to it."

"This was my last record on this contract," he said seriously to Nick. "I'll give you a call when I'm ready to do the next one."

"I'm more than interested in the conversation," he answered. Barry gave Kate a kiss on the cheek and walked away. Arlan had already excused himself while they had been talking.

"So you have yourself a manager?"

"He jumped at it," Nick confirmed. "Of course, I made sure I sweetened the deal pretty well. Lots more money and more authority – oh yes, he wasn't going to turn that down."

"He'll make Mickey look like an amateur," Kate told him. "Arlan is hardcore."

"Then I made the correct decision. Are you done here?"

Kate nodded. "Was going to stop at the grocery store and then head home."

Nick walked her outside and to her car. He pulled her to him and kissed her. "I'll meet you back at the house then."

"I'll pick up something special," she said, returning his kiss. "We can celebrate."

"That we will, love," he agreed. "That we will."

* * *

"What is your problem, Kate?" Nick asked, exasperated at what appeared to be Kate not being able to play the new song. The notes were off and she was struggling to read the music. It just wasn't like her. This was the last song Nick needed to complete his record – things were not going well.

"It's not my friggin' fault, Nick, that you don't hire a company that knows how to write music. A two year old on a toy piano could do better," Kate retorted, storming out of the studio, the sheet music in her hand.

The rest of the guys were doing their best not to laugh, but it was contagious, and soon all four of them were laughing. "And just what's so bloody funny?" Nick asked, in an irritated tone of voice.

"The look on your face is priceless," Andy said finally. "It's good to know Kate hasn't loss any of her sass being married to you."

Nick shot Andy a dark look and said, "Let's go on without her. She can lay the keyboard track later."

Nick and the guys were able to lay the rest of the instrumental tracks while Kate was gone. Some of it was a little harder as this last song had a large keyboard presence but Nick just wanted to get this done. It irritated him when people took a long time laying down tracks. If his stuff went much more than a month, he'd be uptight and cranky toward the end. So far, they were only to the one month mark. This was a big album for Nick — number thirty in his career.

"Let's take a break for lunch," Nick said. "I'll go calm Kate down and we can finish this after you guys get back."

"I don't know that calming is a good idea," Dave replied. "I sure wouldn't want to be on the receiving end of her temper."

Nick ignored the comment as the guys filed out of the studio. Kate was usually quiet and mild mannered, but she did get feisty when she was mad. He followed the guys out of the studio and Andy made a motion back to Nick, pointing to one of the other sound studios, indicating where Kate had gone. Part of him wanted to take Dave's advice and head off to his office. He was sure there was a mountain of paperwork on his desk, even with Arlan to do most of the daily work. But for Kate to explode like that she had to have been fairly frustrated with the music. Because of how well she played, he was leaning toward the comment she made that the music hadn't been arranged very well.

Nick watched Kate from the sound booth for a long time, before deciding to enter the lion's den, as it was. Kate looked up when the door opened and glared at him, not saying anything.

"Go away, Nick," she said finally. "If you want to finish this album today, you need to let me correct this garbage. "

"What makes you think its garbage, love?" Nick asked.

"Listen to it," Kate said, going back to the section that had given her the most trouble. She hummed the melody and played the notes on the page. Nick started to get a strange look on his face as she went through about fifteen bars. "See what I mean? It's almost like a new song in a new key. This is the same crap Ramsey had going on last month."

Nick picked up the music with her corrections on it, looking at it. "You think this will fix it?"

"I have no clue, Nick," she answered, still frustrated, taking the sheet back out of his hand. "But I need you to get lost while I work on it. Being in the same room with you messes with my concentration."

Nick smiled. Kate's words told him that she wasn't angry with him and all was still well in their world, even if she did explode at him in front of everyone. He couldn't be angry with her – that was part of what they had discussed numerous times before getting married and even afterwards. Nick was not going to treat her any different than the rest of the band when it came to the music and the tours. If she had a complaint about something, she was free to express it the same as everyone else. And she definitely had expressed an opinion. Nick walked over and kissed the top of her head. "I love you."

"I love you, too. Now beat it."

"Come find me when you are done, love? I sent the guys off for lunch."

* * *

Kate waved him off and went back to the music. When she had gone to help Barry Ramsey on his album, some of his piano arrangements had come off sounding odd. Taking a minute to look at the small print at the bottom, she saw it was the same company he'd used. Once this was done, she would take it back to Nick and see if they could find a better company to do the arrangements. It took her about forty more minutes to get something that sounded decent and she figured she could ad lib the rest if needed. To save time, she went back to the studio and found Nick and the guys had already laid the other instrumental tracks. This left the piano, and, after a couple of false starts, she was able to get the keyboard track down flawlessly. She had Ron Jacobson, the sound guy, play the instrumental parts back and it sounded nice. The vocals were the only things remaining on this last song.

She ran into the guys on her way to Nick's office, where they proceeded to give her a hard time about what had happened. She was used to their brand of humor and was able to laugh it off easily. They said they were going to go lay the backup vocals, so Nick would only have his own left. Kate nodded agreement – she didn't have to go with them since she didn't sing – and stepped into the elevator to go to Nick's office. Kate was also hoping she would be able to grab some lunch soon; it had been a long time since breakfast. Looking at her watch, she was surprised it was almost three in the afternoon.

JEANINE BINDER

CHAPTER THIRTEEN

Terry smiled as she walked into the atrium where Nick's office was located. The atrium was all glass windows and, being on the fifteenth floor, you could see for miles on a sunny day. Terry nodded when Kate motioned toward the door and she walked in without knocking. Nick looked so official sitting behind the desk with mounds of papers everywhere. *If only his dad had been able to see this*, Kate thought to herself. He definitely found his way into a trade – albeit not what his father might have been thinking. It was hard to see him as an executive – her first images were of him standing on a stage singing his heart out and that would be how she would always see him.

"I think I got it, Nick," Kate said without preamble. "But you really need to blast the company who does your arrangements. Barry Ramsey had the same issue when I laid the tracks for him. He had piano music that sucked and some of the bass guitar music was bad as well. "

"I'll get Arlan looking into it," he confirmed. "We use them for a lot of music and if we are getting trash back, it has to stop."

"Do you want to go get some lunch? The guys are in the studio doing the backup vocals now and I already finished the instrumentals."

Nick pushed half of a sub sandwich toward her. "Terry brought me a sandwich - I didn't know how long you were going to be. You're welcome to the other half."

Kate took the offered turkey sandwich and sat down in a chair next to his desk. "What are you planning once this is done?"

"With all the production time, I expect the record to be ready to release either just before, or after, Labor Day. I would like to hit some cities before the holidays... maybe do some more after the New Year."

"Are we planning anything for the holidays?"

"We could spend Thanksgiving with your parents, love," Nick said. "I was kind of kicking around the idea of going to Jamaica with Trevor and his family at Christmas."

"That's a big step," Kate observed. "Are you sure you're ready for that?"

"I think so. We've been talking a lot over the past year and I can see changes for the better. Jamaica would be a nice neutral place. I have a house on the beach and December is a nice month to go."

"I'm not surprised," Kate said laughing. "You have houses all over the place."

"Back to the concept of the return on investment being greater. I like my privacy and don't want to take the chance of the press being around."

Kate wadded up the empty sandwich wrapper and tossed it in Nick's trash can. "You ready to go finish this?"

"I am. Kind of numb though," Nick said, as they walked out the door toward the elevator to take them back to the studio. "Thirty records. I almost can't believe this is number thirty."

"Dave said it best on tour," Kate said, teasing him. "You're a machine."

He stopped in the hallway long enough to pull her back against him and kiss her. "I'll show you a 'machine' later, love," he said, making her laugh.

* * *

Kate followed Nick in as far as the sound booth. The guys had finished with the backup vocals and gone into the booth to watch. Nick had Ron play back the instrumental tracks so he could hear what they had come up with. Nick was smiling as he listened to it — this was not one of his 'normal' songs. He had written it when he first realized his feelings for Kate and it spoke of his amazement and surprise that it was his turn for love. The song was called "Real

Time" and it was a cross between a ballad and one of Nick's harder rock and roll melodies. Ron set up the take, counted off, and the music started again in the studio. And then Nick was starting the lead vocal. Kate was smiling, hanging onto Andy's arm as they watched the legend in action. Nick wasn't the least bit nervous or self-conscious with everyone watching. He smiled at Kate in between verses, loving the way this song was playing. Nick wasn't sure if his fans were going to like it but he planned to release it first. Nick stopped in the middle of the song and waved a hand at Ron.

"It's going too fast, mate," Nick said. "Can we slow it down?"

Ron made some adjustments and Nick sat back on the stool that was in the middle of the room. After about five minutes, Ron piped the music back for Nick to listen to. Nick nodded as he listened and then gave him a thumbs-up, confirming it was what he wanted. Ron set it up again and started the recording. The song was about four minutes long and there was quite a crowd in the sound booth watching as Nick finished the last song for album number thirty. When he was done, there was a loud silence as Ron played it back in his headset and then turned the song into the studio.

"I got it, Nick," he said, as they were listening to the final version. "That's a wrap."

It was bedlam after that. Everyone crowded in the studio to congratulate Nick. He took everyone's handshakes and hugs before leading everyone out to one of the large conference rooms where food and champagne was laid out. The celebration was open to all who worked there and the other band members called their wives – girlfriend, in Trent's case - to come and celebrate. Kate got along well with the wives. Her circumstance was a little off, as she was a band member and a wife, but soon they were all talking and enjoying the merriment. Kate wasn't much of a drinker, nursing a single glass of champagne through the afternoon and well into the evening. The guys, however, were not holding back and the women were making bets as to who would have the largest hangover when this was done. Nick had decided to go ahead and celebrate – drinking a lot more than normal. The finish of a record was always a time for a party and this one was extra special .

* * *

When it was apparent the celebrating was finished, Nick walked to Kate and handed her the keys to his car. She appreciated that he knew he was far too drunk to be driving and she watched while the other wives pulled out their keys as well. Nick got into the passenger side of his BMW and Kate inwardly wondered if he had ever been a passenger in his own car before. Kate didn't like to drive it because of how powerful it was, but she wasn't going to argue with him. He tipped his head back on the headrest and Kate heard a few snores as she drove silently back to their house. She woke him when they were home and he walked upstairs to the bedroom on unsteady feet. She found him later passed out on the bed, his clothes still on. Kate was trying to keep from laughing. This was probably the most out of control she had ever seen him. She was able to pull his off shoes and wrestled with his pants. After, she managed to get him under the covers but didn't bother with the rest of the clothes. She undressed and slid into bed next to him.

The next morning she heard a text come in on her cell, so she slipped out of bed. She put on a robe, picked her phone out of her purse, and headed into the bathroom. The text was from Marilyn Mitchell, Steve's wife. The text made her laugh. *'Steve said to tell Nick he needs to hire a new bass player since he's never getting out of this bed. EVER.'* Kate responded that Nick wasn't awake, but would pass on the message. Kate took a shower and was towel drying her hair when she heard some groaning from the other room. Walking back in, she found Nick sitting on the edge of the bed, lighting a cigarette. He hadn't noticed her standing there – he was holding his head with his other hand.

"Are you all right?" Kate asked in a quiet voice.

"Oh, dear Lord," Nick gasped. "Don't yell."

It took Kate all she had not to laugh at him. It was obvious this was not going to be a good day.

"Marilyn texted and said you need to hire a new bass player. Steve's a goner."

Nick lifted his head to look at her. "Won't need to hire one. Won't be moving from this bed." Nick put the half-smoked cigarette out in the ashtray and crawled back under the covers, throwing the bedspread over his head to muffle the light. Kate hung up the towel and texted Marilyn back. '*No band to hire for. Nick's done.*' She went back into the bathroom to finish brushing out her hair and the phone rang. Looking at the caller ID, it didn't surprise her that it was Cindy, Andy's wife. "Hello?"

"Kate, its Cindy. How are things there?"

"World War III must have happened because Nick has gone underground to his bed," she answered, laughing.

"He must have been in the same bunker with Andy. He's forgotten how to talk. All I hear is some kind of mumbling and something about never leaving his bed," Cindy said.

"Marilyn said the same thing. I heard Nick up in the middle of the night, throwing up."

"Andy, too," she confirmed.

The two talked for a few more minutes before Kate finished the call and put her hair up in its usual ponytail. Glancing over at Nick, who was still entrenched under the covers, she left the bedroom and headed downstairs to the kitchen. She started a pot of coffee and put a couple pieces of bread in the toaster for breakfast. Consuelo had weekends off, so it was quiet in the house. She had just sat down at the breakfast bar when Nick appeared from around the corner. He pulled a mug out of the cupboard and poured a cup of the coffee she had brewed, sitting down across from her. He didn't even bother to put sugar or milk in it, which was how he normally drank it.

"You look like shit, Nick," she said.

"I feel like shit, love, thanks," he answered. "Please don't ever let me drink that much again."

"I seem to recall saying something about four bottles in."

"Yeah, well."

They sat in silence. Kate offered him a piece of her toast which he took reluctantly. "Are we doing anything this weekend?"

"Had nothing definite planned," Kate confirmed. "My parents invited us to their house for dinner tomorrow, if you think you'll be up to it."

"Dinner tomorrow, I might be able to do," Nick answered, with a groan. "God, I haven't been this trashed since my first record. *That* comparison crossed my mind when I was puking my guts out last night."

"Well, you're in good company, if it makes you feel any better. I talked to both Marilyn and Cindy this morning. Steve and Andy are just as hung over as you are. Andy probably equally as bad - Cindy said he was up all night also."

"I'd like to think it was worth it," Nick said, taking a bite of the toast. "This is why I don't normally drink. I've never have been able to hold it well."

"I always thought it was the control obsession you have," Kate said.

"I don't know about it being an 'obsession.' I don't have the patience for laziness and stuff done half way," he confirmed.

"So, how trashed were you that Monday morning in Chicago? That was some pretty nice, single malt Scotch you were power drinking."

Nick couldn't help but grin. "That's why it took me two hours to come over to the arena with you. Hadn't quite cleared the hangover." He put the half eaten piece of toast back on her plate and stood up. "I'm going back to bed, love."

"I am going to go run to the store and a couple of other places. I shouldn't be gone too long."

"Come roust me when you get back?" Kate nodded and Nick disappeared out of the room.

* * *

Nick was better the next day and they spent the majority of the afternoon at Kate's parent's house. Kate spent the time helping her mom in the kitchen. She had never forgotten what they had done for her so many years ago. Her mom, Nancy, had been wary about Kate marrying Nick for the same reasons Kate had doubts. But seeing them together, Nancy always smiled. She did regret that Kate couldn't have children but had resigned herself years ago that there would be no grandchildren. There was still a chance that they could adopt, but it didn't seem like either of them were planning to slow down any time soon.

"Things are well, honey?" Nancy asked.

"Very," Kate confirmed. "Busy though. Nick's planning to go back out on the road after Labor Day."

"He never stops, does he?" she asked.

Kate shook her head. "Not that I know of. Even when we are on the road, he's busy. Songwriting, most of the time – says he gets his best inspirations when he's touring. Maybe because of all the different places he sees."

"I hope he makes time for you."

"He does. I can't complain," Kate said smiling fondly while watching him interact with her stepdad.

Dinner was nice and Kate smirked at Nick when he turned down the wine her stepfather offered at dinner. He shot her a look but Kate could see his eyes laughing. The subject of Nick's thirtieth record came up and her parents were very supportive, congratulating him and treating him like a son instead of the public person he was. That was one of the reasons her husband liked going to their house, because he was able to talk all kinds of subjects with his father-in-law and Allen was becoming the father that Nick's never was. Nick had tried to get him to come and work for the studio to do their legal work, but her stepfather had declined, saying he liked the partnership he was with and liked being out of the limelight. Nick left the offer open in the event he ever changed his mind but there was still no sign of that happening.

As they were undressing for bed, Kate pulled a small box out of her purse. "I have something for you, Nick." She handed the box to Nick, watching his face as he opened it. Inside was a ring - it was white gold, so it looked silver. Two panthers were upraised in the metal, facing each other on each side, with single rubies eyes. Nick was born in July, the rubies were his birthstone. In between the two panthers, was the letter 'M' for Marshall, with a single carat diamond in the indent of the M.

"I knew when you put the ring on my finger what it meant and I also knew that you would never wear one, just based on how fans would react and how the press would spin it. And, so you know, I don't care what hand you wear this ring on. I just wanted to put my mark on you, same as you have done. I had it made like a signet ring. The guys are not going to buy it's not a wedding band, but the fans and the press will."

"I don't know what to say, love," Nick answered, turning the jewelry in his fingers. "This has to be the finest piece of work I've ever seen."

"And the best part is none of 'your' money paid for it. That was important to me," Kate told him, watching as he slipped it onto the ring finger of his left hand, which is where she was hoping he'd wear it. The fit was perfect. "I did not come into this relationship to take from you, Nick."

"And you don't. You give far more than I have ever deserved."

"It's mutual," she said softly. "I love the way we are together. I feel like you've always been there."

"I like that you're independent," he told her. "I don't have to put all my energies into making you happy every hour of every day. Had a girlfriend like that once; helped to put me off of dating and relationships for a long time."

"I know you've relaxed on a lot of things in the past two years, but something you said in the beginning sticks with me. I know under the difficult person you can be, is the Nick I fell in love with. The Nick that could stand there and let tears fall after you came back from London. The rest of it is a product of what you do."

"You are the first person to ever see that," he murmured, moving to stand in front of her. "The real me - not some icon of someone famous."

"I saw lots of famous people when I was working for Michael. They didn't even affect me. The only reason I was nervous auditioning for you was because I knew you didn't normally hire women. I was a longshot at best."

"Best decision I ever made," he said softly, lifting her chin up to kiss her. "Well, second best anyway. Marrying you was the best."

CHAPTER FOURTEEN

Kate was bored. There were only about two months left before Labor Day and Nick was planning to start his next road trip then. Kate didn't want to start a session with anyone because, most of the time, the sessions went well over three months. She also didn't want to have to try to find someone to finish for her. To occupy her time, she'd started sitting in the sound booth with Ron while he worked. He found her a headset and she would listen to what he was doing as he recorded the tracks. After about three weeks, he let her work the board for one of the new artists; he'd been amazed at how much she picked up. Kate was diligent and made sure she was getting things right the first time. Any additional takes were not because of anything she had done.

They were in the studio doing the tracks for the band, Great Escape. The instrumentals were finished and they were working on vocals. Unfortunately, the lead singer for this group was Christian Long, Nick's drummer about six years ago before he decided to go out on his own. Trent was his brother and Nick hired him with a recommendation from Christian, agreeing to a contract of three records with his band, once he had heard a demo of their music. The other four band members were reasonable to work with but Christian was a nightmare. Biggest problem was he was too much into the drug scene and usually showed up on a big high, which tended to put him off his game. Kate didn't like the man and had no clue how he had ever ended up working for Nick because her husband would never have put up with this attitude. Nick wasn't into drugs – he told Kate he had done them early in his career and didn't like the way he felt when he was high nor did he like the feeling when he was coming down off of that high. Kate attributed his dislike to the control obsession Nick wouldn't admit to having. He did *not* like not being in control of a situation.

Arlan came into the booth and whispered something to Ron which caused him to stand up. He told Kate to go ahead and set up the next take so that things would be ready when he got back. Five minutes later he came back in looking upset.

"What's the matter, Ron?" Kate asked.

"My wife was on the phone. Her dad called to tell her that her mom passed away. I need to leave and take care of her."

"Go ahead," Kate told him. "I can finish this for you until Tony gets back on Monday." Tony and Patrick were the other two sound engineers - both were away on vacation because the schedule had been slower.

"I'll tell Arlan what's going on," Ron said, and Kate stood to give him a hug.

Ron left the booth and Kate turned back to the studio. They were laying down backup vocals because Christian had not yet appeared this morning. Kate didn't want to admit it but things went a lot faster when the band was here doing stuff and their lead singer was late. Sometimes she wondered if he really was forty because Christian acted like a petulant two year old most of the time.

Since it was lunch time and Christian still wasn't there, Kate dismissed the band for a couple of hours. Randy, the lead guitarist said he would go see if he could figure out what was delaying their lead singer. Kate nodded in approval and went out into the hall. Arlan was there talking to Nick, which didn't surprise her. Nick was funny about things being out of the ordinary and Kate running the sound board for Ron – that would be out of the ordinary. Kate walked up and didn't say anything while they continued their conversation.

"You're a bundle of surprises, love," Nick said turning to her. "I had no clue you knew how to work a sound board."

"Ron's been teaching me," she confirmed. "I didn't want to take a session because you want to leave in three weeks or so. You hold the record for the shortest recording time and I didn't want to start something I couldn't finish."

"You good to run this while he's gone?" Arlan asked. "I can call Tony or Patrick back."

"I can do it," she assured them. "I did most of the tracks on Marlena St. Clair's album we finished last week. And there won't be much work to do if Christian Long doesn't get in here."

"Trouble?" Nick asked.

"Nick, he's a pain in the ass. I have no idea how he ever worked for you - not with your attention to detail."

"He wasn't into drugs then. This is the last record we have under contract. I'm breaking even, barely, with his music and have no interest in extending it. Don't tell him that – I'll lay it down to him when his manager comes looking for the next contract."

"I told the band to get lunch and disappear for a couple hours. Randy said he'd go try to find Christian. I was just going downstairs to get something to eat. Either of you want to come with me?"

Arlan declined but Nick agreed it was a good idea. They had a cafeteria on the second floor of the building so people didn't have to go out into the city for lunch if they didn't want to. And it allowed Nick to be free to roam the building with no chance of fan encounters or press barrages. They walked down to the elevator and Kate pressed the button for the second floor.

"Do you like doing the recording, love?" Nick asked.

"Its new and challenging," she admitted. "I could do this part time if you needed me to. I'm still a musician at heart."

"I was just thinking we could open up Studio Four when we got back, if you were going to run the sound board. Good sound engineers are hard to come by."

"That's what Ron said. He told me the last two couldn't cut it."

"It pays more than session work," Nick said teasing her.

"Oh sure," she said laughing as they got on the elevator together. "Bribe me with a new job."

"Did it work?"

"I'll run some of it for you, Nick," she answered. "And, for the record, you don't have to pay me either. Since I'm taking work for Michael, I'd rather spend his cash than yours."

"Not going to get any argument from me, love. Sure that's what you want to do?"

"I'm sure. Besides, I'm going to be really selective about what I take from him and it will cost more than his usual prices."

Nick laughed as they exited onto the second floor. The cafeteria was at the east end and Nick had spent a small fortune to get good food and a nice eating area in place. This was one of the many changes that happened once Nick took over as a half partner, putting his finances in to make it happen. He did the same thing in the New York studio, as well as the one in Britain, both on a smaller scale since both were just recording sets with some offices for the public relations folks. All the main corporate offices were in Los Angeles. In the other two locations, he did a survey of the employees and made a contract with their favorite fast food restaurants to open up in their building. Job turnover came to a screeching halt after that.

Kate put together a salad from the salad bar and Nick got a hamburger from the grill. They sat at a table toward the back of the eating area, to keep Nick out of the way. He wasn't bothered by crowds here, like he would be in a public restaurant, but old habits die hard. Kate didn't mind – she was just happy to spend time with him because this was rare, even with them working in the same building. Kate tried to stay out of his office as much as possible to give him the space he needed to run his business. The important people that ran the studio knew they were married but a lot of the lesser employees – mail staff, general office people, did not. Kate got a few bad looks here and there but didn't let them bother her. Nick was a good looking man and there wasn't much she could do, especially since he was well known.

Once they finished, Nick went back to his office and Kate returned to Studio Two. She was surprised the band was back and even more astounded to see Christian with them. But what she didn't like was how Christian was looking. She had seen that look before in her eight year career and knew he was about to crash. Kate picked the receiver off the wall behind her and asked the operator to find Arlan and send him over. Arlan usually had a radio headset for these kinds of things and she knew he would get there reasonably fast. She tried to ignore the state Christian was in and opened the microphone into the studio to see what they wanted to do. Christian mumbled something and fell off the stool to the floor. Arlan walked in at that moment and ran into the studio. He bent over Christian, making it was apparent he wasn't breathing. Kate saw him radio for help before he started performing CPR. She was frozen in place, watching the scene unfold in front of her. Two of the employees who were EMT certified came running into the studio. Arlan turned over the CPR to one of them and came into the booth with Kate.

"He's not breathing," Arlan said. "Did you call Nick?"

"No. I didn't know how you wanted to handle it," she said, moving out of the way as the paramedics came in the room. Nick was right on their heels.

"What the bloody hell happened?" Nick asked.

"He collapsed," Kate told him. "I came back from lunch and he was sitting there, looking really green, like he was going to be sick. Then he fell."

"This isn't the first time," Nick said in an even tone. "I don't look forward to calling Trent and telling him that Christian overdosed *again*."

"Looks like they got him breathing," Arlan observed. "He wasn't before the EMT's came in."

The paramedics put Christian on a stretcher and walked it through the sound booth, out of the room. Kate could see the rest of the guys packing up their equipment - it was now a waiting game to see if Christian would survive. Nick said something to Randy, who nodded, and the band walked out of the studio. Kate started turning off the equipment and Nick left without saying anything else.

"I still don't know Nick very well," Arlan started. "What will he do next?"

"Christian's brother, Trent, is his drummer; Nick will call him as next of kin. Their parents are dead – Christian raised Trent through his teens and got him the job with Nick when he went off to start Great Escape. After that, your guess is as good as mine. Nick is mad, no doubt."

"Michael always vocalized his... displeasure. It's been difficult learning to read Nick's silent moods."

"Good luck with that. We've been married almost two years and I still have trouble with some of them. This one is easy though." Kate's tone was definite.

"How so?"

"He's mad because Christian is being an idiot. Nick has high standards and I know he wouldn't have put up with the drugs back then. So this behavior has been relatively new. I can tell you this, though, Arlan," Kate said confidently. "If he is angry with you, you will know. Trust me. "

"I hope so. Guess I'll go up and see what he needs me to do."

"I'll finish shutting things down and then I am going to take off. Let Nick know when you go up there?"

"Sure thing," he assured her.

* * *

Arlan went back out, heading for the elevator and pressed the call button with a sigh. He selected the button for the fifteen floor once getting inside and rode it to the top. The scenery was beautiful with the floor to ceiling windows but sometimes the height made him a little dizzy. He stopped and confirmed with Terry that Nick had come back and then knocked on the office door. Arlan heard him call out and walked into the office, closing the door behind him. Nick was on his cell phone.

"I'll go down to the hospital and try to talk to him," Nick was saying into the phone. "I offered him rehab the last time but he wouldn't take it."

Arlan assumed he was talking to Christian's brother, Trent. He went and sat down in one of the chairs in front of the desk while he finished the conversation. Nick talked for another couple minutes and then sat down facing Arlan. "I hate having to make that call," he said.

"Sounds like this isn't the first time," Arlan observed.

"First time here at the studio, but not the first time. Christian has overdosed three times in the past year."

"This time was almost his last. He wasn't breathing when I originally went into the studio."

"Trent is fed up. He said if Christian doesn't go to rehab and kick this addiction he's done with him," Nick told him. "I don't blame him, mate."

"It's a bad deal all around," Arlan agreed. "My oldest got mixed up with crack for a while. It was a hard time getting him to go to rehab and even harder to keep him clean."

"Christian's biggest problem is he has no family support. Trent is all he has."

"That's what Kate said. Oh, and she said to tell you she was leaving for the rest of the day."

"I might follow her after I get done at the hospital. I told Trent I would meet him there in an hour," Nick told him.

"Nothing going on here that you need to stay for, Boss," Arlan acknowledged. "Call me if you need anything."

"Thanks."

* * *

Nick drove down to Cedar Sinai Hospital where the paramedics had taken Christian. Trent was in the waiting room and came over when he saw him. Trent was trying to be angry but Nick could see the anguish in his eyes. He reached over and pulled the man into a hug, knowing how upset he was. Trent clung to him for a moment, breaking away and looking determined. Thankfully the news of Christian's overdose hadn't leaked to the press yet - there were no reporters hovering around.

"Doctor thinks he'll be okay," Trent said.

"He got lucky, mate," Nick said softly. "He was dead on the floor of the studio."

"I am just so tired of this, Nick," Trent said, raggedly. "This is all the stuff he used to say he would kick my ass for if I ever did, and here he is. *Again*!"

"I know," Nick agreed. "But I can't force him go to rehab. He has to want to go and you know it."

"Will you talk to him? The doctor said we could go in but I was waiting for you."

"Sure," he answered, putting his arm around his shoulders as they walked toward the emergency room. Trent gave his name to the nurse at the desk and she let them both in, cautioning them to only ten minutes and telling them what room he was in. When they got to the doorway, Trent turned away – Christian look awful. Tubes were running everywhere and he looked like he had been in a fight. Nick didn't say anything, letting his temper set in, so he could hold his self-control in front of Trent. Christian turned his head as they walked in.

"Trent," he said in a raspy voice.

"You have to quit doing this, Chris," Trent began, a tear rolling down his face.

"I know," he admitted. "This one scared me."

"It should have, mate," Nick broke in. "You were dead for about ten minutes on my studio floor."

"I'll clean up, Trent," he said, as his brother leaned over to hug him. "I promise."

"I'll pay for it, Christian," Nick said. "*If* you'll go."

Christian looked at Nick over Trent's shoulder. "You don't have to do that, Nick. This is my problem - I'll deal with it."

"I already promised Trent. Yes or no?"

Christian nodded. "I'll go. Set it up and I'll go straight from here."

One of the emergency room nurses entered the room and informed them their time was up. Trent gave his brother another hug and walked out of the room. Nick looked at Christian and no words were spoken –the look on Nick's face meant business. He met Trent in the hallway and made their way back out into the waiting room. Nick pulled out his cell phone and called Terry, asking her to get the center director for the rehab center in Malibu on the phone and call him back. His cell rang in about two minutes – Terry was always prompt when he was requesting something. Nick answered the phone and she connected the two men. After he explained the situation with Christian, the rehab was able to get him a spot as soon as he was released from the hospital – which would probably be a couple days. Nick asked for a pen and a piece of paper from the nurse at the desk and wrote down the information Trent would need to get him admitted. Nick thanked the director for his discretion and ended the call.

"Here you go. This is the place I've wanted to get him into," Nick said. "I think it'll suit him."

"I have no words, Nick," Trent said. "Thank you."

"You're welcome," Nick told him. "Let me know if you need anything. I'm going to disappear before the reporters show up."

"I'll be there Monday to start going over the tour stuff," Trent confirmed.

Nick waved as he walked out of the emergency room. He saw a news van pull up and a reporter jump out and head inside. He couldn't help but think how lucky it was he had escaped without being seen. Climbing into his BMW, he headed for his house. The car had Bluetooth and he could make hands free phone calls from the steering wheel. He called Kate to let her know he was on his way.

"Hello."

"It's me, love," Nick said.

"How's Christian?" she asked.

"He beat it one more time. Doctor said he'll be fine."

"He has someone in heaven watching. That boy was stone dead on the floor earlier."

"He finally agreed to go to rehab. I made the arrangements before I left so he couldn't change his mind," Nick confirmed. "Hopefully, it does some good. We can only hope."

"I'm sure Trent is relieved. Where are you now?" Kate asked.

"Almost to Long Beach. I should be there soon."

"Good. Today's been a really long day."

"Won't disagree with you there, love," Nick said, hearing something in her tone of voice. "You've something in mind?"

"You bet," she said softly. "Most of which includes your sexy body."

"Better hope I don't get a ticket," he said laughing. "My speed went up another ten."

"I have dinner in the oven. I thought we could have a quiet evening."

"Dinner might be quiet," he teased. "Lots of noise later."

* * *

Kate laughed with his comments, glad she could hear he was over the incident with Christian. Some issues lasted longer with him and she never knew which way he would go. Kate found it was easier to stay with general conversation and not get too inquisitive until she had established his mood. The fact he called her in the first place was a good indication things were going well. They didn't normally drive into the studio together so they would get home at different times. If Kate was recording tracks for someone, it could be well into the evening before she got home. She cherished the times they had, like tonight. A simple dinner, some conversation, and the time they shared in the bedroom. *Doesn't get any better than that*, she thought.

CHAPTER FIFTEEN

The new tour started off without a hitch. Nick continued to play for sold out crowds even with the shows they did in Canada. Instead of declining like other singers or groups who had been in the music world for years, it seemed Nick was as popular as he had been in the early days. His records had quit selling only at gold level over five years ago and now the platinum records had become double platinum, which were two million copies; one had gone diamond, which was over ten million. The latest one immediately went platinum in the first week of its release and the single, "Real Time" was still sitting at number one on the Billboard chart, even after almost two months. It had become almost common to have extra shows added now just to accommodate the demand. The guys growled good-naturedly that they were starting to spend more nights on the bus than ever before. With Arlan running the day to day business, Nick's phone calls had dropped to only two a week - and this was to check in and make sure all was running fine.

Kate had finished drying her hair when her cell phone started ringing. Looking at the caller ID, she noticed the phone number was strange – obviously not a US number. She didn't know of anyone who would be calling from out of the country but answered it, hoping it wasn't some crank caller.

"Hello?"

"Kate?" the voice on the phone said. "This is Trevor, Nick's brother."

"What's wrong?" Kate asked instantly. She was surprised it was Trevor - she wasn't aware that he even had her cell number but figured Nick must have given it to him.

Trevor paused for a moment. "Is Nick with you by chance?"

"No. He's gone down to one of the local radio stations to do a promo for the shows here in Minneapolis," Kate told him. "What's the matter?"

"Our mum died," Trevor said, almost a whisper.

"I'm so sorry," Kate said sympathetically. "Are you all right?"

There was another pause on the phone. "I will be, yes."

Kate could hear the hesitancy in his voice. It was the same tone she would hear from Nick and Kate knew there was more going on than what was being said at face value. "What else, Trevor?" Kate asked. "You have to tell me. I'm not going to spend two days trying to pry this out of Nick, because he's a bastard on tour with normal issues."

Trevor gave a little laugh. "A little blunt, aren't you, Kate?"

"It's the truth. Nick's one of the hardest people I've ever worked for and musicians in general tend to be fairly arrogant. Being married to him doesn't fix that - it only helps make it easier to deal with his moods."

"Mum died last Saturday," Trevor said, starting to explain. "Phillip didn't tell anyone and I found out this morning when Catherine called me."

"Today is Thursday. She died *six* days ago and your brother didn't call you?' Kate asked, stunned. "I understand why he didn't call Nick, but I thought you two were close."

"Not since Nick and I started to patch things up. Last time I talked to Phillip he called me all kinds of names and hung up on me. That was about a month after I saw Nick in London."

"So his wife called you this morning?" Kate confirmed.

"Catherine said that she didn't think what Phillip did was right. He took care of all the arrangements, did no funeral service, and she's already buried in the cemetery plot with my dad."

Kate didn't say anything for a moment. "Your brother is a vindictive asshole," she said in a definite tone. "This is going to be really hard on Nick. Your mom was the only reason he came for your dad's funeral."

"I know. How long before you think Nick will be back?"

"Probably an hour or so. When he gets here, I'll call you back and hand him the phone. Work for you?"

"I've cancelled my classes for the rest of the day, so I'll be waiting for it."

"I'm sorry, Trevor," Kate said again. "Losing a parent is never easy and I know you've lost both of yours in a short time."

"I appreciate that, Kate," he answered and they finished the call.

Wonderful. After what had happened at his dad's funeral, Kate had not picked up any kind of respect for either of Nick's brothers. She was still working on this with Trevor because he and Nick were trying to lay down a foundation they never had before. They talked at least a couple of times a month – a little less now since Nick was on tour. But this was almost heinous in Kate's mind. *To not tell any of your immediate family their mother died?* She was thankful Trevor was going to tell him because this would not be something she wanted to relay. Both sets of her parents had been loving and kind. Her stepfather was wonderful – sometimes even more loving than her own father had been. But her dad had been sick most of her pre-teen years and they hadn't been able to enjoy a comfortable father/daughter relationship.

Nick was back in about an hour, as Kate had guessed he would be. He was in a pretty good mood which told her the radio interview had gone well. Nick didn't like doing them – he liked the radio ones better than the television ones – but knew he had to sell his music however he could. It wasn't usually necessary because his shows were already sold out but he would keep tickets for the radio stations to give away which always made the fans happy.

Nick walked into their suite with Sam talking about tonight's show. Kate made eye contact with Sam and motioned for him to go back out of the room. Sam made a quick excuse and left. Kate pulled out her cell phone, walking over to Nick. She dialed Trevor's number, got him on the phone, and handed it to Nick. Nick looked confused but took the phone from her, walking into the bedroom.

Kate didn't walk in while he was talking to his brother but was half listening from the sitting room. When it was certain the call was finished, she took a deep breath and walked into the bedroom. She found Nick sitting on the bed and sat down on the bed beside him. She gently put her hand on top of his that was resting on his thigh, giving it a tight squeeze for support.

"Trevor tell you the whole story?"

"Yes," Kate said. "I feel bad because I badgered him to tell me. I was afraid you would keep it locked up inside and I would have to nag you to get you to tell me. I didn't want to do that. You have enough stress while we are out on the road - you didn't need me in your face. "

"I'd like to say I can't believe Phillip would do what he did, but I can believe it," Nick said quietly. "It does surprise me he excluded Trevor."

"From the sound of things, Nick, you can only be on one side. Phillip's or yours. Trevor didn't like the way Phillip was acting toward you and made a stand. He told me he hadn't spoken to Phillip in over two years."

"Trevor's going to do a memorial service there at the college and broadcast it live back here to me so we can be a part of it, albeit remote."

"That will at least provide a little closure for you both," Kate agreed. "Are you okay?"

"Do I have much of a choice?" Nick asked. "I know my mum missed my dad badly. They'd been married over seventy years. That's a long time to be married to the same person and I don't wish her back. And this will let me close the door on the whole animosity thing with Phillip. I've spent the better part of forty years not talking to him. Can easily do another forty."

"It's sad things are that way, Nick."

"Indeed. Off you go, love. I would like some time by myself for a while if that's all right."

"It's fine. I'll tell Sam to keep folks out." Kate stood up and left the room. Going out into the hallway, she found Sam waiting by the door. "Nick's mom died," Kate told Sam. "Nick said he needs some time to himself."

"I'll keep people out," Sam agreed.

"I'm going down to the lobby to call my parents."

"Take someone with you," Sam said.

Kate found Jake talking with Mike by the elevators. She told them she wanted to go down to the lobby to call her folks and Jake agreed to go with her. Kate didn't think it was necessary but it was futile to argue with Sam.

The lobby of the hotel was spacious and Kate made her way to the business area, where the Wi-Fi signal was better, and called her parents. Her mom was home and Kate told her about Nick's mom's passing. Nancy was shocked when she told her what his brother had done. After the call to her mom, Kate went over to a computer and sat down. After about twenty minutes, she had what she was looking for. Phillip had done an obituary for his mom – he hadn't included that she had any other family other than Phillip's immediate family. Kate picked up a pencil off the desk and wrote down the name and number for the newspaper in London on the notepad next to the computer. She picked up her cell phone and called the newspaper.

Being around Nick for two years had rubbed off on her as she was able to understand the thick Cockney accent of the girl in the obituary department and was able to make clear there were some things missing from Tessa Marshall's obituary, asking for it to be edited and sent back out. The girl at the newspaper – her name was Maggie – took all of the information Kate gave her regarding both Nick, Trevor, and Trevor's family. Kate glossed over Nick, not making a big deal out of his name and Maggie offered to email her the new copy. She gave Maggie her email address and while they were still talking, the new version came over her phone. Since Kate had a smartphone, she was able to look at it while talking to Maggie and thanked her for her efforts. Once off the phone, Kate logged into her email on the hotel computer and printed a copy to take up to Nick. She planned to email it to Trevor as soon as she got his email address from Nick.

Once upstairs, Kate headed to the general room and found Nick there, in conversation with Mickey. Kate was glad he had left solitude behind and was back among everyone in a short amount of time. Kate handed the email to Nick before going over to pour a glass of ice tea from the pitcher that was on the counter. Nick and Mickey finished their conversation and Mickey left to go execute whatever they had been talking about. "What's this, love?" Nick asked.

"It's a copy of the revised obituary that's going to run tomorrow in the London Daily Telegraph. It seems your brother forgot your mom had two more sons, two more daughters-in-law, and four more grandchildren."

Nick shook his head. "Trevor will be pleased. I think he's more torn over what Phillip did than my mum's passing."

"I have the electronic copy too if you have his email address," Kate told him. "Trevor is caught in the middle between you two. But I'm thinking this is going to shove him the rest of the way over the fence into your court."

"He called back a little bit ago. He set the memorial service up for nine tomorrow morning, our time," Nick told her. "Sam said it won't be any problem to broadcast it up here."

Kate came up behind Nick and rubbed his shoulders, trying to work out the tension she knew was there. "Are you doing all right?"

"You keep doing that and I'll be asleep, love," Nick told her. "I'm fine. I was prepared for her to go. She didn't sound too good the last few times I spoke with her. I am, however, more than a little pissed at Phillip."

"You should be. That was a horrid thing to do."

"And I'm worried about Trevor," Nick told her. "He's taking this really hard. He's going to see about taking some time off and spending a week with us while we are on tour. I told him he could come see what the rest of the world does. He's been steeped in academia since he was eighteen."

"He'll probably run back screaming; this is not for the weak of heart," Kate teased.

"Not that whole obsessive thing again."

"He laughed when I said you were a bastard on tour. I don't think anyone has ever been that forthcoming with him."

"I try not to be," Nick said, petulantly, muttering under his breath.

"You can't help it, Nick. You didn't get where you are now by being meek and indecisive," Kate said, reaching down to hug him. "I love you."

"I love you, too," Nick said. "This was so much easier than when my dad died."

"I think Trevor being here will be good for you. I'm glad you two have managed to work things out."

"It's been a long time coming," Nick agreed, standing up and pulling her into an embrace. "It shows me a lot of what I'd been missing."

"You're a lot more relaxed now than when I first met you."

"We can be more relaxed later, you and I," he said suggestively, raising his eyebrows at her. Kate laughed and he kissed her softly. "I have empty sheet music that isn't going to write itself. Am going to get on it," he said, hugging her once more then walking out of the room.

* * *

The memorial service went off without a problem the next morning. Nick, Kate, the rest of the band, all the security, Mickey, and even the road crew were in the room to watch it. Nick was surprised at everyone being there, especially the road guys because Nick didn't have much interaction with them. Usually they had things set up when Nick and the band went to do the sound check and were long gone to the next venue before the band even got out of bed in the morning.

Trevor had done an awesome job setting this up. It was held in the chapel at the College of St Mary, on the campus of Oxford. From what could be seen from the camera, it looked like there were over a hundred people in the church for the service.

Nick was quiet before it started, taking in everything that was being broadcast back to them in Minneapolis. There were lilies positioned along the aisle with the pews and at the altar in front of the church was a framed picture of their mother, taken about twenty years ago. Nick could make out Trevor, his wife Shelley, and their four children in the front pew. The rest of the people gathered were a mix of faculty and students, as Trevor had been teaching there over thirty years. He was a big favorite with his students – his English classes were normally full and he had a low dropout rate. Trevor had been appreciative Kate corrected the obituary and had called the newspaper back to add the location and time of the added service.

The vicar gave a moving service. There was not a dry eye in the room with Nick when he had finished extolling the virtues Tessa Marshall had. He talked about her love for her family and had given highlights from her life. As the camera panned through the attendees, Nick suddenly sat straight up, the anger starting to form on his face. Nick got up and went over to the jacket he had hanging up by the front door and pulled his cell phone out of the pocket. He typed something quickly and then came back to sit down next to Kate.

"Nick?" she whispered.

Nick nodded to the screen. "Phillip is in the back row. Bastard," he whispered back.

As the service ended, the camera showed people leaving and the broadcast faded. Everyone in the room with Nick came over to give their condolences, grip his shoulder, and just show unity with him. Nick continued to sit there, waiting for Trevor to text him back while Kate helped to clear everyone out, including herself, leaving him with his thoughts. The message Trevor sent back simply said "I will handle it" and that was all. Nick didn't have to wait long as the phone call came within twenty minutes of Trevor's last text.

"Marshall," Nick said, answering his cell phone.

"I understand things a lot better now, little brother," Trevor launched without any other greeting.

"What happened?" Nick asked. "You get into it with him?"

"That's putting it mildly," Trevor answered. "I'll give you the unabridged version when I get there Sunday. Shelley finalized everything and I should be in Milwaukee by two in the afternoon."

"I'll send Kate to pick you up. I try to stay out of airports as much as possible."

"I can imagine. I'm looking forward to it."

"Me too."

CHAPTER SIXTEEN

Kate and Sam were at the baggage claim at Milwaukee's Mitchell airport, waiting for Trevor's flight to arrive. Kate was getting used to either Sam or Mike always being around. Before marrying Nick, security didn't get clingy until you went to the venue where the show was being held or if you went into town to do something; then they would be close. But with Nick, one of the two men were always nearby, even during downtime at the hotel. After marrying Nick, the extra protection spread to Kate. Nick tried to explain she might be a target for love-struck fans who saw her as a threat. Kate tried to argue things were no different than when she was just his keyboard player, but she lost that fight before it started. If she had a preference, she would choose Sam over Mike, only because she knew him better; Sam always had Brock on her side of the stage, so she was more than covered.

The flight showed on time, so they were casually sitting on a bench waiting. Sam was telling her about his four-year-old daughter learning to play the piano. Kate said that was when she started learning to play and figured out really young it was what she wanted to do when she 'grew up.' Working for Nick wasn't what she had in mind when she was four – she regretted the time lost, not being able to play the classical pieces, but some of Nick's music was equally as complicated. Things had definitely worked out much differently then she'd imagined as a child.

People started coming down the escalator to the baggage claim and Kate easily recognized Trevor. He looked so much like Nick that it almost was him, although Trevor was not as tall and had a full head of graying hair. She saw him smile and accepted the hug once he got to her. Kate reintroduced Sam to him – she knew he would remember him from when their father passed, but it was habit. Trevor only had one bag and it came off the luggage claim conveyor as one of the first bags. Trevor declined when Sam offered to take it and they walked to the limousine that had been waiting for them.

"Limo service, even," Trevor commented as they got into the car.

"Get used to it," Kate said smiling. "It's either the bus or a limo with Nick. Depends on whether we're going from the hotel to the venue or the next town."

"This is going to be so strange for me."

"It's something you have to love. The work is too demanding otherwise."

"So you don't get a break being married to Nick?"

Kate started laughing. "Not that I've noticed," she told him. "You doing all right? I know it's been chaos the last few days."

"It's getting better," Trevor admitted. "The excitement of hopping on a plane and coming here is still there."

"Your bridging the past has done wonders for Nick. It's been thinning the wall he keeps around himself all the time."

"So he's not a bastard all the time?" Trevor asked, teasing her, remembering their phone conversation.

"You get a couple hours free," she answered, with a smile.

The limo pulled up in front of the hotel and one of the bellmen opened the door to let them out. Sam got out first and put a hand out to help Kate, then Trevor. Kate linked her arm with Trevor's to help ease his nervousness – the Pfister Hotel was very opulent. It had wood trim all through the lobby and was beautiful to just look at how the furnishings were arranged. There were twenty-three floors and Nick had the entire eighteenth reserved. Once on their floor, Kyle came over, handing Trevor a room key, took his bag for him, and Kate led him over to the large suite the band was using as a general room. Kate opened the door to the room, holding it as Trevor followed her inside.

* * *

Nick stood up and walked over, the two brothers embracing like the world was coming to an end. Kate moved to the couch along the wall to give them space; it seemed like forever before they broke apart. There were two chairs facing the couch and the two men sat down. Kate had a big smile on her face – it was more than obvious this was going to be a good reunion.

"This is really nice, little brother," Trevor said. "No cheap motels for you anymore."

"Not in a long time," Nick answered laughing. In the early days of Nick's career, there were a lot of not-so-nice motels.

"The part he's not telling you is the entire floor is reserved," Kate inserted. "The whole concept of that still blows my mind."

Nick shrugged. "It's easier if security doesn't have a bunch of unrelated people on the floor."

"It's still nice," Trevor confirmed. "How many more nights are you here?"

"Tonight - we're headed for Chicago in the morning. That's only about two hours which means we'll be leaving late in the morning." Nick paused for a moment. "So, what happened with Phillip?"

Trevor rolled his eyes. "I never could understand why he was so hard on you. I originally thought it was because Mum doted on you so much, being the youngest and born after we were in our teens.

Thought maybe there was some jealousy or something."

"Wasn't Mum," Nick said. "He wanted to be like Dad. His approval was everything."

"And it wasn't until our confrontation outside the chapel that I finally understood what it was that drove him," Trevor said, pausing for effect. "Defiance."

"Defiance?"

"You would never conform. Dad was always on you about something."

"You don't know the half of it," Nick told him, grinning. "You and Phillip were both long gone when Dad and I had our yelling matches. He would've kicked me out of the house had I not gone on my own when I turned sixteen."

"And my mending fences with you, Phillip viewed as an act of defiance because I was standing up for what he thought was wrong. At the service, I pulled him over to an alcove, out of the way. There were over a hundred people there for the service, most of them my colleagues and students; I didn't want a yelling match with all of those folks around."

"Somehow I don't think you managed to avoid that," Nick answered, his tone slightly sarcastic.

"We didn't," he confirmed. "I won't give you the play-by-play. Let's just leave it that he said he had no family, now that his mother was gone, and was very vocal about it. I stared him down for about two minutes and walked away without a word."

"That surprises me, Trev. You were always together against me."

"But I accepted your defiance against Dad. He'd made it clear he wanted all his sons to finish school and be 'respectable.' There was to be no deviance from that."

"I hated school," Nick admitted. "I did okay, but I didn't get the straight A's that you both got. Mostly because I didn't care - I knew I wasn't going to college. Music was all I was interested in."

"Dad cared, though. And that's what has been behind Phillip's anger all these years."

"I wasn't lying to you guys when I said Dad and I had worked this out," Nick said evenly. "He admitted I was dedicated to what I did and that was admirable. Even though I didn't turn out to be a banker... or worse."

"Phillip can't argue your success. He just prefers to hide behind a wall that isn't there," Trevor said. "Oh, and I got a text from Shelley before I boarded the plane; seems Catherine packed up and left him."

"She should've done it forty years ago. He's been a bastard to her since day one. No clue how, or why, she put up with it for so long."

"You do strange things for love," Trevor said.

"I won't argue," Nick said, holding his hand out to Kate, and pulling her onto his lap. "Sometimes love does strange things for you." Kate smiled as Nick hugged her against him.

"Well, I do have something exciting to tell you," Trevor said, smiling as he watched Nick. "The English chair at UCLA is retiring in May. The university offered me the job and I accepted last week."

"So you're moving to Los Angeles? That's fabulous."

"I was hoping you'd be pleased. I see it as a new leaf in the book of life. I want to be where I have family and it seems California is it."

"It will be nice having you close; I've been a long time without family. You and Kate are all I care about." Kate whispered something to Nick and he released her, watching her walk out of the room.

"I was hesitant at first. Moving to a new country, new customs and such. I have tenure where I am and it's a big jump," Trevor confided.

"I can understand those feelings. But I fell in love with this country as soon as I set foot on it," Nick declared. "I had to keep a green card here for five years; after that, I was working toward US citizenship because I wasn't going back to England if I didn't have to."

"Shelley and Missy are excited. The other kids don't want to leave college to come right now, but I figure they will during breaks. At least Jonathan and Alicia will. David has his own apartment."

"I think it's great," Nick said, glancing up at the clock on the wall. "We have about an hour before dinner and I need to take a shower and change for the show. You can hang out here or go to your room — either is fine."

"I need to call Shelley and let her know I arrived in one piece. Where do I meet you for dinner?"

"Back here," Nick told him. "Kate left to get ready because it takes her longer. I don't even try to go in to the city to eat; it simply isn't worth the hassle when I get recognized."

"You know, I never really thought about it that way," Trevor said, walking with him out of the room. "All the success, money, fame, and you're a prisoner to your hotel room."

"That about sums it up," Nick answered smiling. "It's not quite so bad when I'm not on tour. Kate and I manage to go quite a few places - Los Angeles is a big place. But I still limit where I go there as well."

"Thanks for having me, Nick," Trevor said, stopping at his room. "This is going to be a great week."

"I think so too," Nick agreed, gripping his arm, then walking into the room next to his.

* * *

Nick, Trevor, and Kate got in a limousine to go to the arena. Sam, Brock, and Kyle also rode in the same car. Sam rarely wasn't at Nick's side for a performance and Brock seemed to have adopted Kate as his personal charge, which was fine with Nick. Kyle was there because he was assigned to Trevor. Nick explained to his brother how his shows worked and how security was vital to the process. He explained Kyle's job and what Trevor could expect. As much as they looked alike, Nick didn't want any fans to mistake them or have Trevor get into a situation he wasn't expecting. Trevor, however, didn't seem pleased with Nick's arrangements.

"I don't need a babysitter, little brother," Trevor commented when Nick finished.

"You're looking at this the wrong way," Nick said. "I love my fans but they can mob you in a second and the outcome is never certain if you'll get out with your skin. The resemblance between us is too great not to have security on you the whole time."

"It seriously gets that bad?"

"It can, yes. Doesn't happen much these days but only because I have excellent security. And you're not going to like this, Trev, but you have no choice."

Trevor shook his head disapprovingly. "Sounds high-handed."

"I've been doing this for over twenty-five years. A good show is one which goes off without anyone getting hurt and nothing breaking. I can't always help the equipment but I *can* keep my people safe. Tonight, you've become one of them. It'll work out for you in the end anyway, because once we get to the arena, my focus will be on the show and this leaves you with someone to show you how things work."

"It still smacks of babysitting," Trevor grumbled.

"Call it whatever you want, big brother," Nick answered with a smile, as the car pulled into the arena parking lot. "Bottom line, it's my way. No discussion. Ask anyone in this entourage and they'll all tell you the same thing. I should have warned you before you flew all the way out here, but it's how things have to go."

The driver took the car through the underground driveway which allowed entertainers to go inside without any interference from the public. The car pulled up to a single door and the second limousine, with the rest of the band, was right behind them. Security got out of both cars and took over, making sure everyone got out and through the door which led to the dressing rooms. Because they normally got ready at the hotel, Nick didn't have to maintain a separate one for Kate at any of the venues. As soon as everyone was inside, Nick, Sam, and Mickey left the room as Trevor sat down beside Kate.

"Okay, I concede," he told her. "The first word on my mind was bastard."

Kate started to laugh. "You didn't believe me, did you?"

"I thought you were exaggerating a bit," he told her.

"He was being nice," Kate offered. "If my advice is good for anything, Trevor, do what he says. It is not worth the argument... you're going to lose anyway."

"I'd never thought of him this way. He's always been distant around me, but I always attributed it to the fact we didn't get along, even when he was a kid."

"Your brother is one-hundred-percent a perfectionist. He knows how he wants things and it is how it will go. Any deviance from this and you start praying his anger won't be directed at you; there's nothing worse than Nick being upset with you. I'm not any more immune than anyone else in this band, just because we're married. Personal and professional are two different things here and the last thing any of us want is to ignite Nick's temper."

"Are his fans really as big a problem as he makes them sound?"

"They can be. But Nick has learned a lot in this business over the years. That's why he uses the security he does and why things go his way. Just stay close to Kyle tonight and everything will be fine. Kyle will find you a good place to watch the show and you won't have to deal with Nick."

"I'll do that," Trevor confirmed. "I'm learning so much about my brother I absolutely never knew."

"He has his quirks," Kate answered, smiling. "And, for the most part, things work just fine for us. We don't disagree often, mostly because we don't have the 'normal' things married couples argue about. Money is definitely not an issue; I have no clue what he's even worth. Between recording and touring, we don't have much idle time where anything else could be a problem."

"Well, after the whole debacle with Phillip, I took the job in the States to put some distance between us. I'm hoping to better this one with Nick."

"My parents live in Westwood," Kate told him. "They live in a fairly nice neighborhood about fifteen minutes from the university. If you want, I can have them check if there are any houses in their neighborhood. This will give you some familiar faces because I can guarantee they'll be happy to meet you. They love Nick."

"That would be fantastic. Shelley, Missy, and I plan to come during Christmas break to start looking."

"Nick will be home through the holidays. We don't go back out on the road until after New Year's. I know he'll want to help out."

At almost eight, Mickey walked back in and signaled for everyone to follow him out to the stage. Kate followed the rest of the band and Kyle stepped over to Trevor, showing him where he could be backstage. The band got on stage and the crowd started to roar. After a few minutes of making sure the sound was correct, Andy started to count to four and the band started with the introduction music they played at the beginning of each show. After about three minutes, Mickey walked out on the stage and introduced Nick.

* * *

Trevor was mesmerized watching the show. Kyle had gotten him a barstool from one of the lounges and the two of them watched from backstage where Andy was to the right, behind Nick on the stage. Kate was behind Nick to the left, Steve and Dave were toward the middle, and Trent was behind them all on the drums, on an upraised platform. The music was louder than Trevor normally liked but he found himself enjoying his brother's show. He had seen Nick play years ago at one of the local London clubs. He hadn't gone backstage or let Nick know he'd been there – their relationship was bad in those days. He knew Nick had been talented, although he never expected him to be this successful. Their father was extremely negative about Nick's career choice and made it easy for both older brothers to adopt the same position. Although, based on the recent issues with his elder brother, Trevor was starting to regret the time he had missed with Nick.

Trevor liked Kate's idea of her parents checking for houses in their neighborhood – this was one of the things he was nervous about: coming to a new country and not knowing what kind of neighborhood he was moving into. *Was it nice families or was it gang-infested like he had seen on the telly sometimes?* And, even though Kate was young enough to be his daughter, Trevor enjoyed his sister-in-law. She didn't pull any punches and was an endless pool of knowledge to help him get to know Nick better. Catherine, on the other hand, had always been aloof at family gatherings; Phillip being well-known in the banking industry, Trevor felt she thought she had an image to maintain. Their two sons were no different – both went to good schools and had jobs with their father. Phillip's sons were almost Nick's age – Phillip married Catherine when he was twenty and Nick was four. Martin was born within nine months of the wedding and William the following year.

Trevor's kids were younger – David was twenty-one, Jonathan was nineteen, Alicia was eighteen, and Melissa – Missy for short – was ten - so the cousins were not close, either. Trevor wondered if Nick and Kate planned to have any children – Nick was getting close to fifty, so if they were going to start, it should be soon. Somehow, he didn't think they would – Kate seemed comfortable on the stool, playing behind Nick. Nick had told him she was talented – he got to see how much so when she did the solo parts on the ballads. Kate played the piano parts beautifully and, even from where he was seated, he could see pride in Nick's eyes as he turned toward her to watch her play.

It was chaotic after the show and Nick had mentioned they might not be in the same car going back to the hotel. Trevor found himself with Kate but also with Trent and Dave. He asked Kate if this was normal for them to be separated and she nodded, telling him after the show, everyone got into the nearest limousine and sorted it out back at the hotel. Nick was usually off the stage first, so Sam and Mike would move him to the front car. Each night was different, she told him.

The week went by fast and Trevor was sorry to leave. It had been a good time for them both – Nick had told him he felt they had made good headway into building a better relationship. Nick also had lots of ideas for houses for when Trevor and his family came back in December. Nick had been talking about going to Jamaica during one of their last phone conversations, but Los Angeles was just as good for Trevor. He was excited about the move and looked forward to the holidays with Nick.

EPILOGUE

Everything about this Thanksgiving was good. It was the first Thanksgiving in the States for Trevor and his family; it was the first holiday Nick got to spend with his family since he was a kid; and Nancy had found a new best friend in Shelley and an almost-granddaughter with Missy. Luck had it that there was a house almost directly across the street from Nancy and Allen, which, as soon as Trevor and Shelley said they liked it, Nick bought. Nick's argument was because they weren't US citizens, the bank wouldn't give them an easy time and Nick hated the idea of them renting. Trevor tried to argue about it, but Nick wouldn't budge, putting the deed in his brother's name. Kate had been correct – her parents did like Nick's brother and his family and they had become fast friends. Missy made a new friend with Christy, who lived next door and was her age – everyone was happy.

Nancy made dinner at her house – Kate came early with Nick to help – and it was an awesome feast. The food was delicious and not much was left when it was all done. When everyone finished, Nick ushered everyone into the den where there was a piano in one corner, the one Kate used as a kid learning to play. Nick had brought his guitar and Kate sat down behind the piano.

"We want to try something out," Nick said to everyone. "Something we've been working on for a bit."

Nick started to play a soft ballad-style tune and, after a couple of minutes, Kate joined him. As he started into the second verse, Kate could be heard echoing his lyrics. This was new for Kate; she'd never sung with his band and this was something Nick had coaxed her into trying. The song was about finding love and everyone sat mesmerized as they played a perfect duet. The reaction when they were finished was exhilarating – everyone loved the song and Nancy had tears in her eyes.

"We are going to take it into the studio next week," Nick told them. "Plan to release it as my next single."

"It's beautiful," Nancy said, coming over to hug Kate. Nick smiled at the exchange. "I've never heard you sing before, Kate."

"Nick's got all kinds of ideas if this works. We wanted to try it out on family first." Kate added.

"So the plan is we'll get this recorded and then be off for Jamaica. Everyone is still good with leaving on the twentieth of December, right?" Nick asked.

Everyone nodded approval. Kate's parents had originally tried to back out, thinking Nick would want to be alone with his family. Once Nick found that out, he had a long talk with both of them and the subject became closed. Nick wanted this trip to be a *family* trip – not just his, but Kate's as well – because family was what made him happiest these days. The love he had for Kate, the now solid relationship with his brother, and the parental feeling he got with his in-laws. And, for Nick, it was all real time.

ABOUT THE AUTHOR

Jeanine Binder grew up in a small town in California on the outskirts of Palm Springs, where the Hollywood celebrities liked to vacation. After thirty years, she packed up, moved to Arkansas where she still lives today. Writing has always been a passion and hoping the next twenty years will bring many enjoyable books for others to read.

You can connect with Jeanine and find information about her other books on her website at www.JeanineBinder.com.

50629762R00155

Made in the USA
Charleston, SC
03 January 2016